THE SPACE WE'RE IN

KATYA BALEN
Illustrated by LAURA CARLIN

BLOOMSBURY
CHILDREN'S BOOKS
LONDON OXFORD NEW YORK NEW DELHI SYDNEY

BLOOMSBURY CHILDREN'S BOOKS
Bloomsbury Publishing Plc
50 Bedford Square, London WC1B 3DP, UK
29 Earlsfort Terrace, Dublin 2, Ireland

BLOOMSBURY, BLOOMSBURY CHILDREN'S BOOKS and the Diana logo
are trademarks of Bloomsbury Publishing Plc

First published in Great Britain in 2019 by Bloomsbury Publishing Plc
This edition published in Great Britain in 2020 by Bloomsbury Publishing Plc

A catalogue record for this book is available from the British Library

ISBN: HB: 978-1-5266-0194-0; PB: 978-1-5266-0197-1;
eBook: 978-1-5266-0195-7

4 6 8 10 9 7 5 3

Printed and bound in Great Britain by CPI Group (UK) Ltd, Croydon CR0 4YY

MIX
Paper from
responsible sources
FSC® C020471

To find out more about our authors and books visit www.bloomsbury.com
and sign up for our newsletters

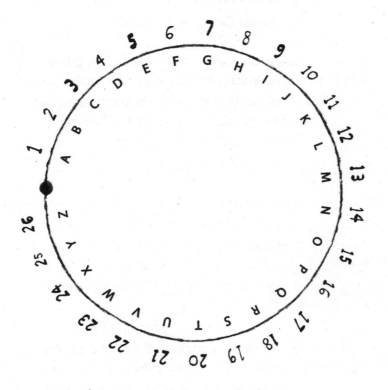

For my parents, and for Patrick

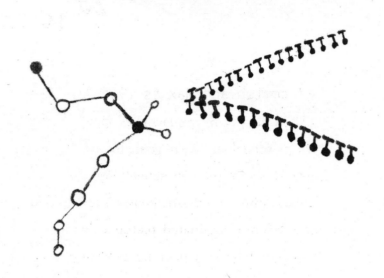

13 5 12 20 4 15 23 14

I am ten and Max is five.

There are twenty-six days until Max
starts school and we're going to buy
new shoes for the new school. We've
looked at his hard plastic book with its
little Velcro-y laminated pictures that
show him what's happening now and
next. It has a blue silky smooth strap so he
can wear it round his neck when we're not at
home and he needs to know what's going to
happen. He doesn't like the weight and the
click-clack of the plastic pages though so Mum
carries it for him instead. Mum showed him the
pictures of shoes and the shop and we whirled

around the world on Google Street View trying to find the shop to show him so he's prepared but it's not there so she's worried worried worried. I went to Egypt on Google Street View and I showed Max but he was jumping up and down so he didn't get to look at the pyramids. Now we are in the car. *New shoes new school* Mum says to Max. Max doesn't say anything because he never says anything and he doesn't stop humming even though I ask him to stop humming.

I'm not going to a new school but I'm getting new shoes. I think that might be confusing Max, so I tell him that I'm not going to a new school. *You are* I say. *You're going to a new school*. Max keeps humming. I tell him to shut up and Mum doesn't say *don't tell your brother to shut up, Frank* because she's worried about the new shoes new school.

We get to the shoe shop and Mum parks the car too close to a wall so I have to wait in my seat while she gets Max out. She puts his reins on and I say *giddy-up* but she doesn't laugh. Max flaps his

2

hands and Mum shows him his special book and I say *new shoes!* but Max doesn't like that. Mum tells him words using her hands, she says *new* and she says *first shoes, then biscuit* but Max isn't looking so he can't listen.

We go into the shop and Max is still humming so people look at him. I used to tell people he was talking but I don't say that any more. The shop is big, too big for Max. I don't see anyone I know and that makes me happy but it's not the sort of happy that makes me smile. I go and look at cool shoes with high tops and long laces and I hold them up and Mum doesn't say no because she's telling the shoe lady that she can't touch Max's feet but that Mum thinks they're a size two. The lady says she'd like to measure Max because they don't like to sell shoes that don't fit and wouldn't it be easier not to have to bring them back? Mum smiles but she's not smiling really, and says that she just wants the same shoes Max is wearing but bigger and if we have to come back we will just come back.

Max is humming louder and louder and his hands are flapping down by his sides and not up in the air so

I think we might have to go. Mum talks to Max with her hands and gives him a ball to squish with his hands because that might stop them flapping. I am still looking at trainers with ticks and not school shoes because I won't get them today because Max doesn't like this.

The lady isn't happy and she says to Max to come here so she can have *a little look-see* at his feet. I want to tell her to shut up but I don't want to say anything at all so I just look at all the tick trainers with high tops and I choose ones with blue laces. I pick them up and check the size and it's perfect for me. The shoe-shop lady says *lots of little boys don't like having their feet measured* and she's *sure he'll be fine*, and that *he's a brave boy and there are stickers for brave boys* and *does he like football* because she has football stickers and *does he play football or support a football team or perhaps he likes Match Attax cards because little boys like those a lot, don't they?* And then it's too many words and Max is having his meltdown.

I don't know why they call it that, because when

something like ice melts it pours itself into a puddle and it isn't hard any more. When Max melts he's the hardest thing in the world and you think he's going to explode his bones from his body. He bites and bites and bites at his fists and his humming is a scream from his chest and nose and mouth. He is fury and he's lost himself and everyone and everything and everywhere.

All the people in the shop are looking at the furious biting boy even though they're grown-ups and it's rude to stare and the shop lady doesn't say anything any more. I don't stare. Mum is using her hands again to say *finished finished finished* and she says it with her mouth too. She picks Max up because he is stiff and small and not a puddle but he kicks and lashes and twists himself *hisssss* like a snake. His fingers are in his ears because he doesn't like the sound he's making and then the two of them push out through the door and Mum holds his reins as he gallops.

I put back the tick trainers with blue laces.

Finished finished f i n i s h e d.

5

3 18 19 19
15

Mum is very cross with the shoe lady but she doesn't say that to me. I am very cross with the shoe lady because she talked to Max when he was tightrope balancing and she pushed him off and down down down. *We'll try again* Mum says. *We'll try again another day.* I know that she means Dad will go and get everything and Max will stay at home and spin himself round and round until he's too dizzy to do that and then he'll watch something else spin round.

Mum takes out the special sticky Velcro-y pictures of shoes from Max's special book and she puts them away in a plastic folder that's fat with pictures he doesn't like and then she gives him his special toy bug that buzzes gently when you touch its nose.

Max has lots and lots of special things.

He has
His special book with
plastic pages and laminated
sticky Velcro pictures to show
him what's now and next
His special plastic
pictures that Angelique is
teaching him to exchange for
things he wants
His special box full of
things that light up and spin
and glow like
his special squashy balls
and glitter tubes and buzzy
bugs to help him
feel calm.

CROWN

OWL

BIRD

HAT

doll

Light House

TREE

SUN

EYES

Smoke

LAMP

BEE

FISH

TRIANGLE

butterfly

TAXI

FEET

Gate

RECTANGLE

SHOES

TOILET

EAT

fruit

SPIDER

drink

LADDER

Table

I have

My football trophies

My bright red bike with

twenty-one gears

My books on detectives

and codes and space

A lock on

my bedroom door.

When he gets home from work Dad goes on his own
and gets the shoes. I stay at home in my room because
he wants to be *quick about it* and Max stays at home
and spins. Mum pushes her fingers into her temples
like she always does when her head is bursting.

Max gets the same shoes as always and forever and
mine are black with laces that give my fingers rope
burn and I wish they were different.

7
12 21
5

There are twenty-one days before school starts. Max hasn't been to proper school before. When he was three Max went to nursery but he melted and melted and melted day after day after day. His face was always puffy from crying and from hitting himself until the skin around his eyes was painted with blue bruises.

Then Max bit another child and the nursery asked Mum to come and pick him up. She cried afterwards and Granny M came round and was all capable and calm and put the kettle on.

Granny M is Mum's mum and sometimes I think it's funny that Mum still has her mum who comes round and makes her tea. Granny M is like a little bird with twiggy arms in soft jumpers and legs draped in grey trousers but she's like steel underneath sometimes, like when people stare at Max or when I haven't done my homework. Mum told her what had happened at nursery and I listened even though I was pretending to be working on codes in my notebook. Ahmed and Jamie and I had a whole new alphabet made of spikey symbols and dots and lines and I was trying to push all of the new letters into my head so I could write them secret notes in class. I put my face very close to the paper so I wasn't even looking at them but I didn't write a single word.

Mum was hiccup-crying in little bursts and she said that Kelsey from nursery wanted extra training before she could be Max's worker again. Mum kept saying *he's never bitten another child before, not even Frank.* And I thought about the little pink and purple thumbprints on my arms from when Max is too excited or too hot or too cross and I didn't really think it mattered about the not-biting. Mum was trying to swallow tea but she couldn't make it go down right and Granny M gave her a thump on the back and Mum cried again and said she was too upset to even swallow a cup of tea and *if you can't have a cup of tea in a crisis then what's the point of being British*. And then she did a laugh that still sounded like a sob. Max didn't go back to nursery after that and he and Mum were stuck together like glue.

18 1 13

19 8 1 3

11 12 5

There are twenty days before Max starts
school and I am in my room listening to him
shout and whirl and melt. The sound is bouncing and echoing up through the floorboards and so I
climb up and up the winding attic stairs until
I can't hear his howls. The stairs creak and
whine but it's because we live in a ramshackle
house. That's what Dad calls it and he rolls the r
round in his mouth and lets it fly out with a
flick of his tongue. Max laughs when he says
it so he says it a lot. *My wife and my boys in
our ramshackle house.* Dad made it sound
beautiful, so when I looked up ramshackle on
Google and it said *in a state of severe disrepair*

I thought I must have found the wrong word.

The house has got strange crumbly bits and the walls lean in towards us and the floorboards groan when Max spins. The top room all the way up the attic stairs has a musty damp smell when it rains but no one but me goes up there now anyway so it doesn't matter. The front door is bright red because Mum and Dad let me choose when I was five and I loved red, and all the leaning-in walls are covered in framed pictures that I did at nursery and some pencil scribbles by Max when he was a toddler that Dad says are definitely modern art. There are pictures that Mum did too, before she had us and lost the time she used to have all to herself.

She was an artist before she had Max and this damp-smelling room was her studio because she said the light from the slanted windows in the roof was perfect. She painted the universe. Stars and skies and great galaxies that change and shift every time you look at them until sometimes they look like something very far away and sometimes they look like something you've known all your life.

She used to have exhibitions in galleries and people would pay lots of money for her paintings and every time she sold one Dad would open a bottle of champagne and they would dance round the kitchen and drink from tall thin glasses. Once, she dipped her finger into the glass and put it into my mouth so I could taste it and it p o p p e d

and burned and fizzed

and they both laughed when I stuck out my tongue and cried that I didn't like it. Then Mum put her arms around me and lifted me high up towards the ceiling and the three of us danced in a circle on the cold kitchen tiles.

When I was small, even smaller than Max, Mum still climbed these stairs in the morning while I played spaceships with Granny M or Dad or the nanny whose name I can't remember. Mum started the day in a clean blue shirt, always a soft blue shirt, and every time she came back down the stairs there were all the colours of a new painting decorating her clothes and her skin. Dad always wore a suit made from something scratchy and dark, with a shirt that stayed clean all day and sometimes a tie with pointed ends like a snake's tongue that he could flick into an impossible knot.

Before Max, he'd always be home to tuck me into bed and he would read me stories about an adventuring astronaut floating through the Milky Way in a crow-black sky, and about the boy detective Tintin who solved puzzles and codes to solve crimes. I loved those stories because all the clues fitted together at the end and then everything was OK. Dad told me when I was old enough he'd teach me a special type of code for computers because that's what he does all day at work but I'm old enough now and I'm still waiting.

Then Mum's blue shirt started stretching out further and further away from her as her belly grew a new person and Mum stopped going upstairs quite as much. Instead she would help me paint paper planets to hang from my ceiling and together we mapped out the stars on my walls. When Max was born she stopped going upstairs at all and she didn't sell any more paintings. Dad started wearing his suit so much it was like it had become stitched to his skin and there were no more bedtime stories because Dad wouldn't be back from work in time and Mum would be with Max.

And now I sit on the floor in Mum's studio surrounded by dried-out tubes of paint that have lost their smell and I scribble my codes on to a huge blank snowy-white canvas. My favourite code is the number-letters-spiral cipher which is just about the easiest code in the universe but it's my favourite anyway. Cipher is just another word for code really but I love the way it sounds. I don't know what the hardest code in the universe is but I want to be the one to invent it. I don't want anyone to be able to crack it, and I'll use it to write everything that burns inside me on days like this.

6

9

7

8

20

There are nineteen days before Max starts
school. Dad has just got home from work and
he promised he'd be home for tea but tea is
finished. Mum and Dad are having a whispery hissed
fight about Max and about *what is best*. Their fight is
the loudest since the time Max gave Mum a black eye
without meaning to hit at all but still hitting, watery
swelling puffing along her cheek and ink-blue teardrop
bruises spilling in a starry galaxy around her temple.

I peep through the banisters while Max sits in his
room and peacefully rolls a marble round and
round a plastic peanut-butter lid. Dad stands
stiff like a soldier but his hands are stuffed
deep in his pockets so that the stitches

make little crackles. Mum throws her arms wide like she's about to give him a hug so big it would wrap around and around him but instead she just starts to cry. She howls that all she wants is to take us away somewhere beautiful. Dad makes these odd little chirrupy shushing noises that sound more like a bird than a man but Mum doesn't notice the birdman standing in her living room. He needs to help her. She says it over and over. Her eyes are swimmy and full and she gulps air like she's drowning.

I don't want to watch any more but I can't move without them noticing me so I sit so still that my lungs start to ache for more air. Mum wipes her eyes and sniffs and says *It'll be OK won't it? I just wish we could get away from all of this*. And in that moment I wish that my piggybank that's shaped like a football had more than eleven pounds and forty-seven pence in it so I could take her on holiday far away from our ramshackle house.

8

5

12

16

There are eighteen days before Max starts school. Dad tells me that he's going to start doing more for me and Max and won't that be nice, a bit more time together. *Mum's been feeling tired, champ, so we have to help out a bit more than we do right now.* He looks a bit guilty when he says this and he starts tugging at his tie so that the knot gets tighter and tighter.

He tries to put me and Max to bed and it all goes wrong. Max's bath isn't right and it never is but Dad doesn't sing the bath song or splash the water with a pat of his hand to show that it's really OK. He doesn't put on the bedtime lightshow that speckles the stars across Max's ceiling and bathes his little face in all of the universe. Everything falls out of place and I sit on my bed listening to the screams that echo from room to room until I hear Mum's soft voice sing a lullaby that rises up over Max's sounds and hushes them back into his mouth.

I brush my teeth and put on my pyjamas and read four pages of my book and have my half hour on the iPad which has a cracked screen from when Max flew it down the stairs *whoosh bang*. I time myself and no one comes to tell me the time's up so I have forty-five minutes instead and then I turn out my light because no one comes to tell me to do that either.

I hear Dad slip out from Max's room and his socks padding on the floorboards outside my room. I pretend to be asleep and he puts his face around my door. I squint through half-closed lashes and through the blur I can see his tears.

20
18 5 1
19
21 18 5 19

There are seventeen days before Max starts school
and Mum and I are going to a flea market to hunt
for treasure. Mum wakes me up early, even earlier
than for school and the sun is painting the sky
with orange streaks. We leave Dad and Max at
the kitchen table eating breakfast and walk to
the train station just the two of us with no
Max strapped into his too-big pushchair
or flapping and bouncing as he walks
next to me and taking up all my
space. It's just me and Mum
and she holds my hand
even though
I'm ten.

At the station she buys me a hot chocolate with extra whipped cream that is piled up like a cloud in the cup and on the platform she talks to me about my favourite things. We talk about space and the universe and how it would take 800 years to fly to Pluto in a normal plane and how the sunset on Mars is blue. We don't have to sing songs or talk with our hands or hold Max's stiff-melting body when the rumble of the train on the tracks makes him scream. When we get on the train she taps our secret code on to the palm of my hand and I tap it back.

Our code is Morse code and it was invented

hundreds of years ago before telephones and texts

and emails but the people who used it then had

machines that tapped out messages made of short

taps and long taps. It was for sending messages to

25

places far away, and you can even do it with torches ♩♩♩♩♩♩ ♩♩♩♩♩ ♩♩♩♩♩♩♩♩♩ ♩♩ by making long flashes and short flashes but Mum and I use it when we're right next to each other so it's special and it's ours. We use our hands and Mum taught it to me when I was little and we were learning to speak to Max with his signs. We all had to learn how to say finished and thank you and biscuit with our hands. But when I was scared or angry or crying or lonely, Mum could take my hand in hers and the taps and lines dot-dot dot-d a s h-dot-dot d a s h-dot-d a s h-d a s h meant she loved me. Just between us.

When we get to the flea market we walk through a world of colour and shapes and noise and we don't have to make it all go away because Max isn't with us. It feels like the world has been switched on. I can smell dust and age and when a man drops a chair we don't have to leave because of the bang. Mum finds me a whole set of *Beano* comics from right back when they started and their pages are yellowed with all the years since they were printed but there isn't a single crease lining the paper. I imagine the child who had them all those years ago being so careful with the delicate sheets that felt like flower petals and I hold them in my hands like they are made of glass.

Mum can spot a bargain at a thousand paces and as she wanders through the tightly packed aisles of people all burrowing through piles of clothes and knick-knacks and ornaments she's the first to spot a glint of colour peeking up from the bottom of a wet cardboard box. She puts her hand in and gently digs down until she frees her prize. She holds a little scrap of light, a luminous orb filled with arches and swirls and bubbles that shine and reflect the whole world around us. Mum says it's a paperweight but it looks like it's a piece of magic to me. It flings out its colours like a magician pulling handkerchief after handkerchief from his sleeves just like the one at Jamie's eighth birthday party. I'd wanted him for my party but in the end we went to the cinema instead and Dad had to stay at home with Max anyway.

When we get home Mum puts the paperweight on

a shelf in my room next to my football trophies and its light bounces off my star-print walls where the constellations swirl and twinkle. My room is somewhere Max can't go and it's full of my treasures. I have a padlock on the outside of the door to keep it locked when I'm out and he's not, and the padlock has a code to open it. It's 2302 because that's my birthday and Max doesn't know that.

Now my room is even better than before. Mum stands back and declares the glass orb looks just right and it's like it had been made especially for our house and for my room. It slots right into its place like a piece of a jigsaw puzzle and I glow inside because it's like magic and Mum bought it just for me and it looks *just right*.

25

18

15 18

19

It is fifteen days until Max starts
school and the sun is peering
pathetically from behind fat clouds.
Ahmed and Jamie are still on holiday
and it feels like they've been away
forever and I'm the only one from our
gang left. I am bored in the house so we
have to go out so I can be bored outside
instead because Mum says being indoors is
making me loopy and loud. I go and see what
Dad's doing but he's working on his computer
even though it's the weekend and he doesn't want
to show me what he's doing or talk to me about
how everyone on Earth would weigh two and a half

times as much if they were on Jupiter or that space is completely silent.

I want to go on my own but Mum says *we should all go out together* and *it'll be lovely* and *it's such a beautiful day isn't it*. It definitely isn't but I wait while she shows Max the park card and then the swing card because he likes that one the most. He flies up higher on the swings than even I can because Max isn't scared about falling off. When Max swings he makes his noises which I know sound funny like a baby and an animal all jumbled together with a laugh in his mouth and sometimes he lets go but he never falls.

We walk to the park because it's just at the end of our road except Max doesn't walk there. He goes in his too-big pushchair so he can't run off and away to find blue cars and red buses. I hate the pushchair because it doesn't look right and people stare at it and then again and then they go *oh*. I have my football so I kick it boom out of the door and I pelt into the summer-hot-damp morning street because no one will stop me. I run past Mr Next Door who is actually called Mark who studied art at university with Mum and now they live right next to each other and *isn't life full of coincidences?* When we moved here Mum said she saw Mark and they each did a little double-take jump that meant *I know you!*

Mark's walking his supercool hairy dog who is called Neil. Mark comes round most weeks and he and Mum talk about paint and drink tea and I get to play with Neil and he's the cleverest dog in the whole wide universe. I think Neil is a strange name for a dog but I'd love a dog like him to pitter-patter after me as I zoom on my bike and nose a ball like a doggy football player so I'd always have someone to shoot goals against. Mum says we have enough on our plates without having a dog too so I can't have my very own Neil. Max likes Neil which is weird because dogs make noises and jump about suddenly and Max hates it when people do that.

I reach the park and I sprint past the playground and to the grass that is my football stadium. I dribble and shoot and volley and I am Messi and the crowd around me roars as I score goal after goal until Mum is there and she says *he wanted to walk with you* and I say *he wants the swings* and then I run away again to win the World Cup. There are bigger boys without their shirts on playing football near me. They have shaved the sides of their heads so just a stripe of tufty hair grows on top and I wonder if Mum will let me do that too. I want them to notice my magic feet and tell me I'm the best ten-year-old they've ever seen play football and can they play with me so I can teach them how to be good.

Max goes on his swings and he makes his noises as he flies. The boys are sweating and they look up from their game and they don't look at me even though I'm scoring the winning goal against Brazil but they look at Max and they laugh at his happy swing noises. They use bad words when they talk but then they use the worst word of all about Max which begins with an R and Mum said I could never ever say. Then they laugh and laugh and laugh. And I laugh too. They look at me and I laugh with them and they grin and

say *all right, mate* and I play football with them and I
score while Max swings and doesn't care at all.

After our game the boys lollop off with their shirts around their shoulders and some of them smoke cigarettes and call me a legend.

I walk home with Max and I let him hold my football but he wants to hold my hand so we do that too
and I want to whisper *I'm sorry* but I don't.

33

13 15 14

11 5

25

2 15 25

It is fourteen days before Max starts school. I am
going to be a Year Six. We are top of the ladder, Dad
says. *The monkeys on the highest branch of the tree.*
Max isn't coming to Wolverton Juniors with me.
Mum and Dad talked about all the different
places he could go to school and that they could
have sent him to a boarding school far far away
where he'd have a different bedroom and
someone else would coax him into the bath
and read his favourite stories while he fell
asleep but Mum said no way. Mum and
Dad went to see it anyway and Mum
came back and she still said no way
and so they went to see another

school near us. They left me and Max with Granny M which was OK but Max thought it was strange because he bounced about looking for Mum and flapping a straw in his hand like he does when he knows something isn't the same and he isn't sure about it at all. Granny M's come round quite a lot this summer and she says Mum needs some time to herself. Mum never used to leave Max but once a week she slips out of the door superquiet like a mouse and when she comes back she never says where she's been but she's tired just as if she'd taken Max with her anyway.

Mum and Dad got back from seeing Max's new school and were very excited and told me and Max about a soft playroom and that there was a bubbly swimming pool. I thought that was a stupid thing to tell Max because he hates having a bath but he didn't seem to mind. Mum said *Maxy they have your special toys there and all the teachers can talk with their hands and there's a room of lights that change colour when you press a button! It's like a spaceship!* He put his head on one side and they showed him a new special book called *This is My School* which has pictures of the new school and all his teachers.

There are more teachers at Max's new school than at mine but there aren't as many children. Dad says *they're not all teachers, some of them are for helping children with other things like running or talking.* Max can only do one of those but he's very good at it. I said *he wouldn't need that help* and Dad laughed and then said that he thought *maybe the talking not-teacher would mean Max could say words to us* and not just hum and wail and make the noises he made on the swings.

I wasn't sure if the new school would make Max suddenly start using his words with his hands and his mouth because ever since Max stopped nursery Angelique has come to see Max twice a week and he can't even say c-a-t cat. Angelique is a *speech and language therapist* which sounds scary but she isn't. Angelique comes on Tuesdays and Thursdays and always Tuesdays and Thursdays except when she goes back to visit her family in France but she doesn't do that very much.

When she first came to our house she came right in and sat on the floor right next to Max and just handed him a light-up windmill. My muscles turned to stone and my stomach went swoop because she was sitting there in his air and he needs his space especially from new people unless he's decided he wants to sit on top of you all of a sudden. But Max turned his face to her and took the windmill and it lit up in his hand and he giggled and Angelique said *we're going to be friends, aren't we Max* and Max put his tongue on the windmill so he could check the taste of its colours. Now he waits at the window for her to come twice a week every week and she says he's on the very edge of doing something brilliant.

10

15

25

It's thirteen days before Max starts school. Today is
Tuesday and Angelique is sitting in the kitchen and
Max is sitting too. Max is supposed to give her a
plastic card with a picture of a toy he wants, but
he won't do that yet. It's a swap, a card for
a toy. If Angelique puts her hand over
his and helps him to pass her a
card then he does it but it's
just copying. Angelique
says she has to
break
things
down
for Max and then he'll be able to build it up himself

38

soon. *Break down a task into tiny chunks, Frank. Then he'll learn to put the chunks together again and do it all for himself.*

I know Max is desperate for a ball that has a swirl of glitter swimming in its belly. Angelique has two cards and all he has to do is pick one up, even if it's just the one with a picture of a paperclip on it and not the one with the shiny ball at all. One day he'll be able to pick up the right plastic card and hand it over and then one day after that he'll be able to put up a card that says 'I want' and then add the right card next to it on a plastic strip that he hands over. And then after then he's meant to be able to make all sorts of sentences and hand them to us, but Max won't even do this stupid first bit. He keeps reaching and reaching straight for the ball and I think he might melt right then and there on the kitchen floor and I'm annoyed because I want to get some orange juice. But Angelique puts her hand over his again and guides it down and his little fingers scrabble at the plastic card and pass it to her and when he gets his glitter ball in return he is alight with joy.

Angelique turns to me and says things I find easy like getting dressed or asking for what I want are harder for Max and I think in my head *I know that* but I nod and say outside my head that he needs things

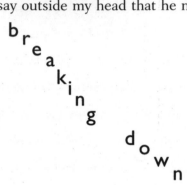

Angelique smiles a lot and nods when I say that and says I'm a good brother and I don't tell her about the football boys in the park because I get hot liquidy sparks fizzing inside when I think about doing things like that but I do them anyway.

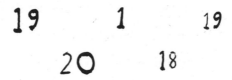

It is eleven days before Max starts school.
Mum tells Max that he's going to wear a T-shirt
with the name of his school on it and she shows
Max the T-shirt but he won't touch it. She puts
it in his drawer on top of his other clothes and
says *it's a nice uniform.* I look at it and it has
stars on it where my uniform just has letters. I
tell Max his uniform is *cool* and Mum and Dad
smile but Max just wants to put the washing
machine on. Anyway there's no way Max will
wear his school T-shirt because he thinks he
only wears one T-shirt. It is grey with
yellow stripes and he has fifteen of them
because I counted.

41

Mum picks up Max's school T-shirt again and she counts the stars with him but he doesn't care. She tells him he will only go to school for the mornings and she shows him morning with her hands and then she says he'll go for the whole day when he's ready. She shows him his clock with the sun and moon and stars and moves the pointy hands with his hands and says it all again. She says the name of his school very s l o w l y and then very quickly and she shows him his schoolbook. Max only likes one book really and it's *The Baby's Catalogue* and I hate it because it's for babies like it says in the name and Max is five.

One day last year Mum pushed Max in his too-big pushchair to pick me up from school instead of me walking home with Jamie and Ahmed. When Max saw me he held his baby book up high towards me and squealed. Noah laughed and said *mate, is that your brother?* even though he knew it was. And I shouted NO and I ran all the way home and far away from Max. I was angry with Noah because Max was proud of coming to pick me up but I was angrier

with Max for being proud and angriest with Mum for
bringing Max to school.

When Max is watching the

washing whooshing round and round

I go and look at Max's new book that tells him all about
his new school so he's not surprised when he gets there.
It looks different and more fun than Wolverton Juniors.
The picture of it from the outside shows a low white
building with round windows and it does look just like
a spaceship. The inside is spaceship-y too with rainbow
lights and shiny sleek touchscreens in the white-walled
classrooms. The book is written like Max is saying it.

I can use the Jacuzzi.

I can play in the sandpit.

I can ask for snacks.

There's a picture of a boy that's not Max and he's
handing over a picture of a biscuit and he's getting a

43

biscuit from a teacher but that won't work because Max doesn't like those biscuits. Max won't like that picture because it's not him and those aren't his biscuits. Max's biscuits live in a red tin with yellow spots and Angelique is teaching Max to ask for them with a plastic card. Max will have to take his tin into school because once Granny M put Max's biscuits in a different tin and he wouldn't eat them because it wasn't right and then he melted. I wanted to tell Mum and Dad about the tin but they were talking with their heads down low and Mum had taken out Max's new uniform and was smoothing it with her hands again and again.

6 21 18 25

It is seven days before school starts.
Mum is reading a story with Max and she
curls up on the floor in the living room with him
and then she shows him new things for school and
does Angelique's homework with him. It takes hours.
She has to print some new Max cards and she has to
make important Max phone calls where her voice
goes low and quick and she and Max are glued
together and it makes my brain go red. Max's squashy
balls and spinning wheels and light-up sparkly sticks
are everywhere and even though they throw glitter
shadows on the carpet I still manage to trip
and fall a hundred times.

When I hit the rug for the hundred

and first time I throw a whirly little plastic spinner at the wall and it cracks and smashes and its silver water streaks down wetly to the floor and Max howls and starts to hit his head like he does when he's melting into fury or when he hears something that makes his brain burn. Mum gets out his favourite thing ever which is thick paper he can't rip and wax crayons which smear their colours on the card and he gasps and he sits and draws things that look like things we know and *he's just so clever like that isn't he* says Mum. *Sit down and draw with us* she says and her hands make quick practised perfect pencil strokes across her paper until there's a Lego man jumping on to the back of a tiger.

I want to see a film and go bowling and swimming and not stay in the howling jungle with this hurricane boy everywhere I turn. I ask and ask and ask and I sing it and shout it and squeak it and shriek it and Mum says *not today not today not today*. Then she snaps and she uses a voice that isn't low but it's very quick and she shouts

46

Frank don't you
ever think about
ANYTHING
how could we do those things with Max?

the noise of the music

and the clunk of the pins

and the flash of the lights

and the splash of the water

and a new swimming costume

and he hates baths you know that

and the dark of the cinema

and the flicker of the screen

and will you just

stop

and think just think about what you're asking

and go and read a book

or play on that stupid iPad

or watch TV

or shoot goals at the garden fence

but will you just STOP.

47

So I STOP
and I go into the kitchen
and I find a red pen
and I draw hieroglyphics and pictures
like the cavemen did
and I write my name
and I try to write how unfair
everything is but I can't make the words click
together into sense so I write all the words that
are bad and cruel and
nasty and cool and I
scrawl and scribble
and I roar and howl and
shriek and fight
but not with

6

my voice and I use the pen
until every inch of wall
that I can reach is a
sketch of the

19

15   18

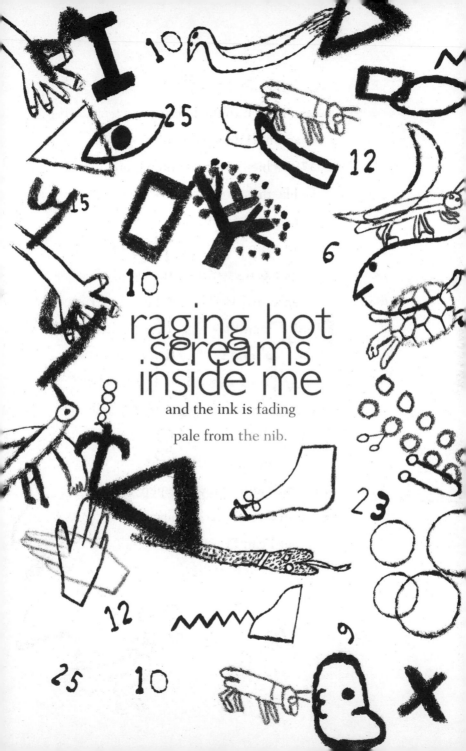

raging hot
.screams
inside me
and the ink is fading

pale from the nib.

Mum goes to make tea and sees what I've done. I hear the sound of a hurled teacup shattering against the wall and I hide in my room with my duvet over my head so my bed is a cosy tent but my heart is thumping in my ears. The stairs creak and thud and there's a shuffle of feet outside my door but it doesn't whoosh open and bounce off my wardrobe like it did when Dad came into my room after I'd poured my chocolate and banana milkshake over the sofa when I was five and they'd brought Max home forever. Mum taps our Morse code on to the door so I know it's her and then pushes it open like nothing's wrong but it's very wrong because she's crying in quiet little coughs and she says *oh Frank I'm so sorry my boy I'm so sorry* and she sits on my bed and she strokes my head even though it's covered in my football duvet and she whispers over and over that she's sorry and I start to curl into her words.

3

9

7

1

13

The next day Dad takes the day off work. We go on a train and leave Mum and Max behind with their books and their stories and his shouting. I feel a funny tug when I look at Mum's tired face and the kitchen walls all scribbled with my fury and I think I don't deserve to go on a train to Brighton to see the sea but Dad gives me a smile that squeezes that feeling out of me.

In Brighton I eat fish and chips from newspaper and they taste like the salted air. Dad and I queue up on the pier to go on rides that make my stomach swoop and I can feel the chips swirling in my tummy. We go on the teacups and I like spinning then, when I can see the world whirling around me and the faces of the crowds being whooshed into a blur. When my tummy is feeling a little bit less swoopy we buy candyfloss and it melts into pink streaks in my mouth and it sticks in bright sticky sugar lumps to my teeth but it doesn't matter at all. Then Dad leans in and asks me with a wink whether I'd like to have some more chips on the beach.

I toe the waves on the beach and the water licks me to shivers so I don't swim even though I had put my trunks on under my trousers in the morning.

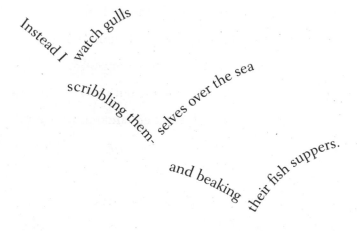

Instead I watch gulls scribbling them-selves over the sea and beaking their fish suppers.

I copy their *caw-caw* call and throw them the last of my vinegary chips and they fight each other for the scraps in an air-beating flap of feathered wings. I do the *caw-caw* again and Dad laughs and tries to do it too but he sounds more like our old cat that yowled around the house asking for food. We walk back along the beachfront and see performers with painted metal faces and robot hands and magic tricks that make Dad give a low whistle *wow*. The pier is a whirl of colours that spin out and dance into new shapes in the splashes of sea between the boards under my feet and that was real magic.

When we get home Max is already in bed and Mum and next-door-Mark are having a drink in the living room. Mark has brought Neil round, and I stroke his grey tangled-fur head and I can't stop talking about the performers and the seagulls and I accidentally tell them that I had chips twice but no one seems to mind at all.

23

9

12   **4**

There are three days before school starts. Things are better because Ahmed and Jamie are back from their holidays. Jamie went to Spain. Ahmed went to Bangladesh. He shows me some pictures on his phone and says *Man it was hot and I didn't even have to wear shoes*. I thought Max would like that and probably Mum would like it too because then she wouldn't have to see the shoe-shop lady again, but my holiday was only one single day and they had more stories.

Ahmed said he'd actu-ally been a bit bored in B a n g l a d e s h

55

because he was with his boring grandparents and aunts and uncles and they sat around in the heat all day and talked and laughed because they don't see each other very much but Ahmed didn't have anything to do except be hot and not wear shoes. Jamie said he'd wrestled a shark in Spain but Ahmed and I just laughed at that. Last year Jamie went to Florida and wrestled an alligator but his brother had just said *In your dreams, mate* when he heard so we don't believe Jamie much any more. Jamie's brother is fifteen and he shaves the sides of his head but not the top and has trainers with high tops and long laces. Ahmed has five brothers and sisters and he's the baby even though he's ten. Neither of them has a Max. I'm the only one with him.

We are all together again but we don't know what to do with ourselves because there's a whole summer between us and it's raining. We go to Jamie's house and watch new videos on YouTube with the volume up and no one says *Jamie turn it down* and we play *Minecraft* and use blocks to build a new world with endless towers and it's better than when it's just me but we are loopy from being indoors.

When the rain stops we go for a bike ride in the Wilderness. It's not really the wilderness, but it's like it. The grass is all scrubby and rabbits kick and jump with velvet legs and the trees are wild and spring out from the turns of the path like in a pop-up book. Ahmed says the trees are thousands of years old and I believe him. Some bits of the Wilderness are bare and open and other bits are dark and tangled and I like those bits the best. Once we tried to build a den in the tangles but we didn't really know how and all we had was a sheet that Jamie stole from his mum, and some sticks that were too small. So now we just swoosh on our bikes and don't stop until our hearts go *beatbeatbeat* too fast and I have to shout *stop!* with the last of my air.

When we are airless we sit in the damp scrub which smells like the rain and hot leaves and a steaming kettle and a bit like Mr Next Door's dog Neil. Today Jamie wants to make a fire and maybe we

can trap a rabbit and cook it and eat it with our teeth and fingers tearing meat and juices dribbling down our chins. We are wild boys surviving in the wild woods. When I don't come home and Dad comes to find me he'll see me living in a den wearing rabbit skins and a necklace of bones and my face streaked with rabbit blood and he'll go home and tell Mum that Frank is a true wild boy and he's not coming back to walls and doors and bedtime and special books and melting. Mum will be sad and she will go and buy me trainers and a PlayStation and she'll cry real tears but I still won't go home.

Jamie has a red plastic lighter he stole from his brother who smokes skinny white cigarettes that he rolls himself. Jamie makes a nest of leaves and twigs and we wait for them to go whoosh into sparks but the lighter won't click and throw out its flame. We don't feel so wild any more because everyone knows you need fire to live in the wilderness and cook rabbits. I think that maybe the leaves and twigs are too damp for flames but Jamie clicks the lighter again and shakes it and then throws it at Ahmed and says *it must be a dud*. Ahmed shakes it and clicks it and a little blue flame flicks its tongue from the silver tip. Jamie doesn't like that and he shouts at Ahmed and Ahmed shouts back and I put my fingers in my ears because I wanted us to be wildboys of the woods together, even just for today.

Then Jamie throws a shower of wet leaves at Ahmed and Ahmed throws a handful of soil back at him and no one is cross any more. We throw great chunks of the forest floor at each other until we're panting and dripping with mud and bits of trees. Ahmed and Jamie look like wildboys and I know I must too. I smear mud on my face and let out a Tarzan-shout that bounces off the trees and fills the damp air around us. Ahmed and Jamie copy, and then Ahmed does a wolf howl that sounds almost real. We shout and whoop and howl and charge at each other like bulls until I feel lighter than I have all summer.

Ahmed tells me and Jamie to go and get the driest twigs and leaves we can find, and by the time we get

61

back he's made a circle of stones for us to put them in. He builds the sticks up so they look like a little triangular house. He says he saw how to do it on the telly and then he takes Jamie's brother's red lighter and Jamie doesn't say anything this time. We all watch with eyes like saucers and faces swiped with muddy warpaint as Ahmed coaxes the flames like they're an animal. They're reluctant and timid at first but Ahmed blows gently on the little licks of fire and they start to roar.

We warm our hands by our very own fire and keep feeding it the dry twigs. It eats them hungrily until we haven't got anything more to give it and it spits and stutters until it's nothing but glowing embers and Ahmed stamps them down with his thick boots until the faint orange fades to grey. Then I take a stick and I scratch 23 9 12 4 into the earth and Jamie and Ahmed and I sign our initials. 10 and 1 and 6.

14 15 20
6
1
9
18

I take my bike and pedal it home so
very slowly away from the wildboy
wilderness. I can see the lights in the
kitchen bright and steady through the
window and I want a spitting hot flame
flicker fire to light me instead. It is time
for tea and Mum and Dad and Max are
sitting round the table in the last glow of the
evening sun and I am on the outside looking in.

I slink into the house like a stealth ninja
because I don't want to sit in the kitchen and eat
with Max and see him taste his food first with his
nose so the smell doesn't surprise him in his mouth.
Max doesn't use a knife and fork or even a spoon

because he won't hold the metal or plastic or rubber without saying no no no but not with words. He eats with his hands in the same way that I am not allowed to and in the same way that wildboy Frank would eat his fat dripping meaty rabbit by the Wilderness fire. But I am not a wildboy and I am not a slinking stealth ninja because Mum straightaway says *hello Frank well done for being home for suppertime* and she's calling me into the kitchen so I skulk in like a hunter stalking prey but she says *is there something wrong with your shoulder?* so I stop and glower and sit down at the table and leave wildboy hunter ninja Frank for another day.

Max has his special plate and I have any plate because I don't mind. Max's plate has Mickey Mouse on it but Mickey's face is all bubbled because Dad put a hot pan on top of it by mistake and Max didn't ever want a different plate even when Dad went and bought the exact same one. Max knew it wasn't right and I didn't know how he could know that. Max likes four foods and they're not healthy and they won't make him grow up big and strong. I told him that he needed to grow his muscles like Popeye and eat spinach but then I thought about Max with muscles and I didn't say anything else about spinach ever again.

Max likes Quavers, mashed potato, plain biscuits and chips with no red sauce. *A good spread of potato there, mate* says Dad when he puts Max's plate in front of him. Sampling the varieties. *Next year we could throw in a roastie, eh?* Then Dad puts peas on the table too but Max never eats his greens because he won't eat any colours. I still have to eat vegetables and I don't think that's fair but life's not fair says Dad and I think that's true or Max would be different.

20 15 15 2 18 9 7 8 20

It is the night before Max starts school. After tea Mum puts out Max's starry uniform and my Wolverton Juniors jumper and polo. Tomorrow I will take my bike to be a Year Six top-of-the-tree monkey and Max will go in a bus that comes right to the door and takes him away to the spaceship with the fizzing lights room and the iPads and the little bubbly swimming pool.

In Max's special schoolbook it says that a lady called Rhoda will help him on the bus and there is a picture of Rhoda and she is old and smiling and wears a bright yellow vest over her jumper and it's like the kind the builders next door wore last year. Max hated those vests because they were loud and zingy yellow. Rhoda's jacket is too bright and it will hurt Max's eyes and he will have to squeeze them tight shut so he won't see Rhoda or be able to look out of the window on the drive to school and Max loves to look out of the window and make his noises when he sees blue cars or red buses because they're the best ones.

I tell Mum that Max won't be able to look at Rhoda and doesn't she remember next door's builders and she does a deep sigh from somewhere sad but nothing else happens. Later she makes me a hot chocolate and lets me drink it in bed but her eyes are faraway and I can't find the words to tell her that I under-stand, just a little bit. So I use our special code and I tap out three words on her palm and she tells me she

loves me too.

6

1

12

12   9   14   7

In the morning it is school and I put on my polo with
its letters and my red Wolverton jumper which is new
because it says Year Six on the back so all the little
children know who is at the top of the tree. I
want to wolf down my cereal and my breakfast banana which I have every
morning before school and
always have and always will and
then cycle fast with Jamie and
Ahmed quicksmart so we can play football in the playground before the bell goes.
There are new cards in Max's special book and they
are *bus* and *school*. Max isn't wearing his starry school
shirt and his hand is red and bitten so I know Mum

has tried. I heard him screaming this morning while I was in the bathroom brushing my teeth and washing my face and I splashed the water in the sink so the droplets flew up and speckled the mirror and I watched the tiny rippling waves instead of listening to the shrieks.

He is wearing his new shoes that look the same as his old shoes so he doesn't know about the new bit and they light up blue in a flash like he likes. I think it's weird that he doesn't notice new shoes but he notices a new plate but no one can ever explain Max to me. He eats his breakfast Quavers and drops plain biscuits on the floor and draws a cat with green eyes and ginger fur just like our old cat that died when Max was three and how does he remember? He looks at the cards in his book and I know he's looking but he doesn't turn his head and look straight at them and instead he looks at them from the side of his eyes and he claps and rocks and he's worried about everything being new new new. I tell him *new school*, and I tell him it will be fun. I talk to him about the room of cool lights and the iPads. Max doesn't want to listen to me and he pushes my words away with his hands and I give up. He's a scaredy boy today.

I can't find my pencil case anywhere at all and I know I left it on the side table in the kitchen. I ask Mum in a quiet voice and then I say it louder and louder until I'm almost shouting but she's not listening. I'm getting more anxious by the minute because I can't turn up on my first day in Year Six without the right things.

A minibus pulls up outside but it's not red so Max won't like it. There aren't as many seats as the coach I went on for the Year Five trip to the Science Museum where everything was something and you could touch anything without being in trouble and I thought that Max would like it here except for all the noise. I got him an ammonite from the museum shop, an arching swirl of frozen history and Max loves to run his thumb along its ridges.

I can see through the window that there are other children on the bus already and some of them are all wrapped up in strange seat belts that look like the tangled trees from the Wilderness. Some of them have their fingers jammed into their ears and some of them are stabbing at iPads without looking up at all even though the bus has stopped and the driver has put the hazard lights on so that the orange flashes through the window and bounces around the kitchen.

Mum says they're early but I know they're not actually because I can see the big orange kitchen clock. Mum's fussing and getting all the things she thinks Max needs and Max is trying to show her his picture of his cat but she still isn't listening to me and I still haven't found my pencil case. So I clamber and stand on a chair to stretch up tall to shout out loud so she'll see me and hear me for just that one moment. But Mum doesn't look up at me so I wave my arms in the air. The chair has a leg that sways and wobbles side to side so it's not for standing on but I am Frank the monkeyboy who can climb to the top of the

highest monkey-puzzle tree and I am Frank the
wildboy who wears rabbit skins and swings from vines
shouting out a wildboy cry and I am Frank the
spaceboy who jumps from asteroid to asteroid at zero
gravity. Then Mum sees me and she gasps *Frank* and
I
am
Frank
ordinaryboy
and then I turn and then I

                  t

                    u

                      m

                        b
                       l

                         e

And then there are biscuits everywhere and I land on
them and they go Crunch and my arm goes
crunch and Mum goes *Christ*.

4

15   15

12

2

Mum calls for Dad in a voice I don't know
and he runs in with shaving foam icing his
face and his tie isn't a tie because it's not tied.
The doorbell is going trring trring
trring and I am on the floor with my arm
full of stinging bees and the biscuits scattered
and the chair upside down and suddenly but
not really suddenly my head is all syrupy wet with
blood. Max is starting to flap his hands like a
broken bird and the doorbell rings trring
trring trring again and Dad goes
Christ. Mum says *help Frank, do something*
and then she runs to the door and a lady says
you're really supposed to bring them out, are

you having some trouble? and I think that must be Rhoda and I think that my arm looks like Sam's arm when he fell off the swing and it's all loose and alien.

I am thinking too much and not at all because everything has happened and nothing is happening. Mum is in the kitchen with a lady who is Rhoda from the picture and her vest is very yellow and Max covers his eyes and does a wail song. I want to say that it's too bright but my teeth are stuck together and I might be sick.

Dad is holding whimpering Max in his arms and he's saying *Frank Frank Frank* and I think he might have been saying it for a long time. Rhoda will think we're all mad and she is looking at me on the floor with my alien arm and all the biscuits and splashy blood from my head and now Max is a howling animal and Dad is foamy and Mum is doing a hiccup-cry, but Rhoda says *oh dear* and she takes off her vest and turns it inside out and says *well I can make that better, shall we go to school now Max?* and she says it with her hands and she says it with her mouth and she's

74

kind and we all know that right then. And Max is wriggling down from Dad and taking one of her talking hands and he's trotting like a little horse with Rhoda.

Dad stops saying Frank and Mum stops hiccupping and my arm stops fizzing but I still know it's there. Time isn't tick-tocking at all, except for all around Max as he bouncy trots to the hall and out of the front door and then the spell explodes and Mum rushes out of the door with Max's backpack which has cars all over it in a hundred different colours but they're not too bright and he loves it except for the green and purple ones.

And then Dad is scooping me up which makes me scream from deep down in my belly which is the first noise I've made since I crunched and crashed to the floor and he goes *oh god Frank I'm so sorry* and he puts me in the front seat of the car and when he leans over to do up my seat belt my arm gives a fresh scream of pain and shaving foam drips from Dad's face on to my trousers. The blood from my head drips too and it blooms in the foam like a snowy battleground. Mum gets into the driver's seat and she grips the steering wheel so tightly that the bones are bursting white from her knuckles. Then all of a sudden we vroom in the car to the hospital faster than the speed of light.

2 18 15   11 5 14

Mum says Dad has called work to say not
today so he can stay at home in case of Max
having trouble at his new school and Mum calls
Wolverton Juniors while she's helping me out of the
car and she says what has happened. It sounds cool
when I hear it all pieced together for the school recep-
tionist. My arm is throbbing like my bones are made
of hot metal but I don't mind so much because it's just
me and Mum. I don't mind one little tiny bit that I am
missing before-bell football with Jamie and Ahmed
and probably Sam too.

When we get to the hospital we go to the
waiting room but the lady behind
the desk takes one look at my

77

battleground trousers and my bendy arm and my bloody head and we don't have to wait in that room at all. I've never been to hospital before, not until today. When Max was born I didn't visit him because Mum didn't even stay in hospital for a single night. *Everything went so well*, she beamed, *that they let us home right away.* Mum must come here with Max now for some of his appointments because she knows where everything is and she even smiles at some of the staff but she looks at them the same way Max sometimes looks at people, without really looking. One of the smiling staff says it's nice to see her which is weird but maybe they're just being polite even though they don't say it to me.

Someone put my arm in a white sling that feels like bed sheets and it hurt like mad when they did it but now it feels better cradled in cotton. We are in a little cubicle with a curtain you can swoosh round to make a room and when it's closed people say *knock knock* rather than knocking because there isn't a door. The curtain is covered in lions and tigers and trees and a swoop of sky and little kids might think they were in the jungle but I just count the animals. I get to forty-seven before Mum says something and I lose track of the muddle of creatures. I think she's waiting for the phone to ring and the new school to say come and get this boy NOW but Dad calls and says Max is safely at school and he has to clean up all the biscuits and the blood which is *everywhere* and I think I'd quite like to see because it's like a horror film but in our house.

Mum hangs up her phone and says there's an egg on my forehead and I touch it with my fingers and feel a hot lump of bruise and my hand is damp with a squashed berry smear. The doctor comes and says *knock knock* and she looks at my head and says that she'll glue it up and I laugh and laugh because I think of her fixing me with a Pritt Stick from her doctor's pencil case and Mum says *I think they need to look at your brain you mad thing* and that makes me laugh more and even the doctor says very seriously that I might have laughitis and that there might not be a cure and then she laughs and says she's caught it. My arm still pings and zaps in its new sling but this is fun and I get to have an X-ray. I am excited about seeing my bones and I don't even mind when they have to cut off my new red Year Six jumper with scissors and I see my arm is a fat slug with my skin stretched on top.

Mum walks and I whizz down the hospital corridors to the X-ray on a special bed with wheels pushed by a man called Mick who has a moustache and a tattoo of a lion on his arm. He asks me about school and football and films and then he tells me about how when he used to go to the cinema his mother would give him 50p to buy a ticket for one of the best seats at the back but he'd buy a cheaper seat and spend the rest on sweets. All the sweets had names that meant I could taste them as he talked, like pineapple cubes and aniseed twists and barley sugar and rosy apples and I forget about my buzzy arm and my egg head.

When we get to the X-ray room Mick gives me a wink and lopes away humming into the twistyturny white halls. I am not so excited about seeing my bones now because the lady who takes the picture wants me to move my arm and I can't taste the sweets any more so I remember that it hurts. I put my arm on a silver table and Mum has to wear a funny apron to stop the X-rays zapping her inside but it's not funny enough to stop my arm screaming and the noise comes from my mouth when the lady uses her gentle cotton-wool soft hands to turn my fat wrist. Mum says *be brave Frank, I know you can be brave* and she kisses the top of my head and I cry and cry and cry.

Afterwards it's not so bad because I'm bundled back into the white bed-sheet sling and Mick zooms me to my little cubicle to wait to see my pictures. My face bounces back at me from glass windows and it's all damply streaked with crying but Mick doesn't say anything about that. He tells me about his car which is called Marvin and is older than Dad. Our car doesn't have a name and when I tell Mick that he says Marvin is his baby even though he's got four grown-up children and a dog called Winston.

81

2 15 14 5 19

The doctor shows me my X-ray and the inside of my arm is cloudy grey with shock white lines and one of them is torn through the middle. The bones are reaching for each other and the sharp cut edges should fit together in a ghost jigsaw but they're all jaggedy and wrong and Halloweeny. I really want to show Ahmed and Jamie the X-ray because my arm's definitely broken and that is definitely cool. When Sam broke his arm he had a cast wrapped in coloured stripes and it was rough and heavy and we wrote our names with felt tips and scratched the ink into drawings and he got to referee all our football matches.

I choose bright blue for my cast and Mum shields her eyes and says *you'll blind us all* and we look at each other and laugh but then I'm worried because I chose blue for Max really but I remember Rhoda's jacket. I want to change my mind but the plaster cast man is ready with rolls and rolls of blue bandages. I've had two chalky white tablets that the doctor gave me and my arm aches a bit but on the very edge of all the thoughts I have. The plaster-cast man wraps my arm up lickety-split all quick and his hands are careful and it's neater than a Christmas present and very blue and maybe it's too blue and I worry.

The laughitis doctor doesn't glue my head together because we watched her called away to An Emergency which meant that all the doctors went whoosh out of cubicles and did a funny running walk to a room with big angry signs on the door telling patients never ever to go in unless you're The Emergency but then the doctors would take you there anyway.

A nurse called Sadie fixes my head with a gloopy goo and not Pritt Stick. It hurts but I say it doesn't because Sadie says I look brave and I want to believe her. Mum goes a bit green and asks if I mind if she makes a superquick call to Dad and I think she might be sick so I say *go please go* because I hate sick. Sadie looks at my cut and says I'll probably have a scar but that girls will like it a lot. I don't really care if girls will like my scar because I don't play with any girls and it's Jamie and Ahmed and Sam who will really want to see my glued egg.

Sadie asks me lots of questions about *Minecraft* and sport and all the things I like and I tell her because she's kind and when she smiles she means it. She asks what I want to be when I'm older and I say *I want to be a detective* even though I've never even thought of that before but I like it straightaway because detectives can crack codes. Sadie says *that's a great choice* and she asks if my mum and dad are detectives. I laugh at the thought of my mum in a hat like the one Sherlock Holmes wears and carrying a magnifying glass. I tell Sadie that my dad makes computer codes and my mum was an artist but she's not really one any more and then my voice gets a bit lost. Sadie says that being an artist sounds *so cool* and that she loves to paint when she's not gluing up people's heads. She asks what Mum likes to paint and I try to describe the whirly shapes and splashes of colour and starbright swirls of sky and Sadie seems to understand.

Next she asks about brothers and sisters and I nearly choose to say no but then I say Max. I tell her about his flapping and melting and noises and biting and the word those boys in the park used and the new school. Sadie asks what Max likes to do and I think that's a strange question and so I answer a bit slowly about *The Baby's Catalogue* and the washing machine and drawing but not talking and Sadie nods and asks if Max has a favourite film. It's *Cars* and *Cars 2* and she's all excited and sparkly and says those are her little boy Bobby's favourite films too and he's five too and his favourite thing ever is Spider-Man. She asks if Max likes some other films that Bobby likes and I say he does because he does and then she shows me a picture on her phone and her little boy is just any little boy with curly blond hair and a superhero T-shirt. So I ask her if he's like Max and she says not in the way I mean but they like the same films and she's sure other things too because they're both little boys starting school. I think that doesn't mean anything and they're not the same.

Sadie finishes sticking my head back together and says I can go home soon but not to school today. Mum is still phoning Dad to tell him about my jigsaw bones so I make Sadie promise she will tell Mum I have to go home with her and not to Wolverton Juniors. I'll show Year Six my cast tomorrow.

Mum gets a prescription for me which is a piece of paper we can swap for more chalky white tablets to stop my arm from buzzing and then we can go go go. Another nurse smiles when we walk out and says to

Mum *see you soon* and I ask Mum why and Mum ruffles my hair and says the nurse means when I come back to get my cast off.

Walking feels funny because my bright blue cast is heavy and drags me down like a sucking swamp and I can smell it too. It smells like paint and dust and something sharp but I can't find its name. I ask Mum what time it is because I'm suddenly starving and I tell her I'm hungrier than a hungry hippo and I could eat a horse. Mum says she's not sure if we have any horses in the freezer *but then you never know* and she chuckles.

She looks at her watch which has hands that can light up in the dark without even pressing a button and says it's lunchtime and we can go to McDonald's but *shhh don't tell your father*. I am full of a balloon stretching with happiness inside me but I still have room for two Big Macs and a strawberry milkshake. It's funny only eating with one hand because I haven't ever thought that I eat with two hands and I'm not even using a knife and fork for my burger. I still make a mess and get some splotchy red ketchup on my blue cast but Mum says never mind and calls me a *mucky pup*. We play Noughts and Crosses on the napkins and I show Mum YouTube videos and when I think she's going to say we have to leave she gets me an apple pie and I win seven games of Hangman in a row.

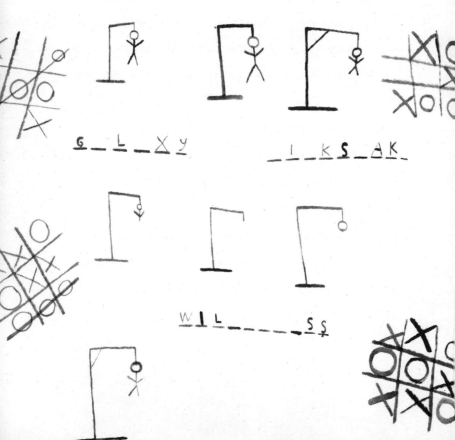

23 15 18 18 25

When we drive home I am full and warm and I feel
better than if I was a wildboy with rabbit in his belly
and a firewarm cave in the woods. Mum goes slowly
round all the bends so my arm doesn't get jolted and
jiggled about and I'm glad because I'm thinking
about my X-ray and how maybe if I move too fast
then the bones will slide right past each other.
Sadie said they would knit together which I
thought was a funny way of saying it because
my bones are not woolly. Sadie also told me
that teeth are bones and I look at mine in
the wing mirror and all the usual little
white squares in my mouth are
suddenly wrong and I don't

want my tongue to touch them. Then Mum wonders how Max's first day was and her lips smile but her eyes are tight with worry and I forget about my boneteeth and worry too. She runs her hands over the blue silk scarf wrapped round her short hair.

Mum used to have really long hair that ran in a black river all the way down her back. She brushed it so hard that it crackled and shone and when she was thinking hard she would twist it up into a coil above her head and let it fall down in a silky waterfall. Max used to love her long hair and he would whimper and cry if he couldn't put his hands in it and run his fingers through every hair and wrap it around them. He wasn't always gentle, and when Mum told him no he would melt and scream until he could soothe himself again with the strands. A few months ago Mum went to the hairdresser and came back with her hair chopped short and it was like a whole new person was in our kitchen. Max didn't eat for three days afterwards and he kept pulling sharply on the new hair as if he had to check what was missing and it hurt her. So now Mum wears a scarf or a bandana wrapped up tight and Max is starting to forget.

Dad opens the door to us and he gives his long low impressed whistle-wow at my arm and at my head. He holds me by the shoulders and takes a good look at my egg and says *and did they tell you what to do if your head falls off? But seriously, thanks for the day off work, I owe you, mate* and I giggle and Mum hits him with the paper bag of chalky white tablets.

Max is in the living room sitting on the floor and he's wearing just his spacepants and his grey and yellow stripes. Max wears spacepants because he is scared of the toilet and the whoosh of the flush and the water that appears from nowhere. Max doesn't call them spacepants and they're really a nappy but they have planets printed on them and they're for bigger boys than babies. I don't tell anyone about them. Max is looking at his *Baby's Catalogue* and watching TV and using one hand to squash a ball that looks like an eyeball. I bought that ball at the school fair but not for Max so it's mine but I don't say anything. I look at Max's face because then I think I'll know what happened at school. His skin is so pale it glows ghostly but that's Max and his eyes are dark with bruisey tiredness under them but that's Max too. There are no actual real bruises or angry red raw teeth marks printed on his hands and so I think it might have been OK.

I say *hi Max I broke my arm when I fell off that chair. I've got a blue cast and it doesn't hurt that much and there's glue holding my whole head together*. Max sideways looks with the corners of his tired eyes and he puts a finger in his mouth and then touches my cast and I think *gross* but I don't move just yet. I am glad it's not too bright and Max wouldn't touch it if it was because the colour would burn his skin. Max feels colours with his whole body and doesn't just see them with his eyes like me. I think that's why he won't eat them at all, ever.

How was school Max I ask and I say *was it good* and I do a big smile or *was it bad* and then I do a silly cross

92

frowny face. Max laughs and he puts his licky fingers on my face and pulls it into a frown again but he's not really answering my question. I get his thumbs up thumbs down picture cards and say *choose!* but he just giggles and grabs my face again and his dribbly fingers knock my glued egg and I shriek like it's cracked. Max hooks his fingers in his ears and his jaw goes CLAMP and twitchy and he's gone far away into another world so I get up off the floor which is quite hard to do with one arm working and the other arm not. I slump on the sofa instead and I put the TV on with the sound down low and for once Max curls up beside me and watches with half an eye.

Mum comes in and says how happy she is to see me and Max together like that and she tells us that we're not just her world but we are her universe and her space and her stars and her sky and her galaxy and her cosmos too just like she always says. She says she's scared to give me a cuddle because I'm all ragtag and falling apart at the seams and I might crumble to dust but she's joking and she cups my face in her hands and

93

gives me a cinnamon hug and it's because she's made my favourite biscuits. They're in the kitchen and they're shaped like different dinosaurs except they got too big in the oven so they're puffy fat beasts with stumpy legs and wobbly spikes. I'm still filled up with apple pie and milkshake and burgers but I eat a biscuit because she made them just for me.

After Max has had his chips and not had his bath and is wrapped up cosytight in his bed Mum shows me a green notebook with his name on it and says it's a diary that his teachers write in every day. It's not written like Max is saying it all which I like and I read about how Max played an alphabet game on the iPad and chose a xylophone from the choosing box and found his name on his peg. No he didn't I think and I say *he can't read*. Mum shrugs and says *he's taken it in somehow and it's only three letters so we made that easy for him*. And I sit in the kitchen where the floor is shining clean after my sticky head blood and I sulk because if Max can do these things there then why doesn't he do them here and just be a normal brother?

19
23
5 5 20 19

The next morning Mum wants me
to stay at home with her and she
says she'll make the sofa into a
nest of pillows and duvets and the TV
can be all mine at any volume but that's
not true because Max will come home at
twelve sharp. She says *we can have a
morning just us two, I'd like that.* And then
her voice goes a bit funny but I've just seen
myself in the mirror in the hall and my forehead is smudgey with a blue bruise that's
blooming like ink in water and there's a split of
red with dribbles of glue meshing its edges and I
think *cool.* I want to go and show my arm and my

bruised egg to Ahmed and Jamie and Sam.

So I wheedle *please please please* I want to be in Year Six and Mum dithers about and she's *just not sure* but then Max squawks a parrot sound and she says *fine fine fine* and disappears to find out why he's being a bird. I get dressed but I don't have a Year Six jumper because the doctor cut it off and I find one from last year which doesn't have anything on the back. I put it in the back of my drawer and squash it down under my pyjamas and socks. I put on my polo and it's hard to get my arm through the armhole, much harder than I thought it would be and it makes me hot and bothered so I definitely definitely don't want to wear my old jumper now and I don't think I could even get it on anyway and I don't want Mum to dress me because I'm not a baby. I go downstairs just wearing my polo and Mum says *where's your jumper Frank?* I tell her and she says *wear your one from last year* but I say it's lost.

I can't bike to school because of my arm so I think I'll have to walk on my own while everyone else shoots past. But when I leave the house Ahmed and Jamie are waiting at my gate and they look at my weird blue arm and they spend ages poking it with their fingers. Jamie taps it and says *awesome* and he makes the word really long and low so I know he's impressed. Ahmed gives me a bag of sweets from his mum because she thinks breaking your arm deserves a treat. I share them with Jamie and Ahmed even though they're for me. They're all different flavours and some of them are so sour that they make our mouths pucker and wrinkle. We stick our tongues out to see if they've wrinkled up and instead the sweets have painted them rainbow colours and Jamie's is bright purple and he looks so funny trying to see it that we can't stop laughing and all of a sudden we're late for school.

Our new teacher is Mrs Havering and she doesn't say anything about us being late. She smiles at me which I didn't think Mrs Havering ever did because she's as strict as a teacher from the olden days and there's a rumour she keeps a wooden cane in her desk to whip and smack at any child who talks when she says *quiet* in a voice that's speckly with ice. She smiles again when she sees my arm and my head and I remember about bones being teeth and then that it was teeth being bones and hers are grey. Mrs Havering says *Frank, it's nice to have you here* and she lets me sit with Jamie even though Eric Morris told me last year that Mrs Havering never lets friends sit together *fact*.

7 15 12 4 5 14 18 1 20 9 15

We have maths for my first lesson in Year Six. I like maths because you can be wrong or you can be right and I get it right. Sums are codes and you can crack them and I am the codemaker and the codebreaker. I whizz through my worksheets and when they're finished I sketch new sums in my brand-new blue exercise book that smells like wood and air. I haven't broken the arm I write with and I think that that might have been cooler because then I might get a laptop or someone else could do it for me. I write my name

F R A N K

as neat and tidy as I can but it slopes down the cover and away from me. I start even bigger sums from my new textbook that cracks like a whip when I first open it. I make the numbers as high as I can but they're not high enough because numbers never end.

After we've finished maths we have art. We're going to learn all about Leonardo da Vinci and Mrs Havering tells us he was an artist *and* an inventor and he drew the plans for a helicopter hundreds of years before we had the technology for them and *how amazing is that?* She puts some pictures up on the whiteboard. One of them I know, it's the *Mona Lisa* and it lives in France and it's in one of my books at home. Another is an old drawing of a man with one head but four arms and four legs and everyone is giggling and being stupid because the man isn't wearing any clothes. Mrs Havering lets people laugh all they want and she just stands at the front waiting and I keep thinking that they'll laugh the lesson away but after a few minutes boredom drains their voices away. Then Mrs Havering says something that snaps my head up lightning-fast. She says *some people say these paintings show us a code that explains the design of the whole universe.*

My codes unlock words and sums and sometimes feelings but they can't unlock the universe because that's impossible. The universe is vast and black and random and bigger than forever and we're all just tiny specks floating inside it. I am staring at Mrs Havering and I'm waiting for her to laugh an icy laugh and say it's all a mistake, a joke, a trick for making her wait so long to start her lesson.

But she doesn't.

The code that connects the whole universe.

I'm leaning forward on my chair, tipping it on to two legs in exactly the way they tell you not to or you'll slip and hit your chin on the desk and bite through your lip or break your arm exactly like I did yesterday but I don't care. I can feel my heart thump-thumping in my chest. *The code that connects the whole universe.* It feels like magic, something that makes the universe make sense and everything that's swirling all around me fit into place.

Then Mrs Havering speaks again. She says it's called *the golden ratio* and it's some measurements and numbers that artists use to make their paintings as beautiful as possible. *Pleasing to the eye.*

All the breath inside me hisses out again in a disappointed wheeze. Art isn't a code. It can't be. It can't be the code for the whole universe. I can't crack art, I can't find a little chink in the sequence to dig down into and burst the meaning free. It doesn't mean anything at all. I write down *golden ratio* in a swirl in my exercise book and it just sits there, flat and still. Real codes leap and rattle and jump on the page when you start to solve them and explode when you crack them.

Mrs Havering is tapping the board. She's still talking about art, about Leonardo da Vinci making this perfect picture of a man using this amazing code and when everyone laughs again I don't care. She says all the proportions of the picture are as perfect as possible so it's absolutely as beautiful as possible to

102

the human eye but it doesn't look like it to me. She tells us that these measurements are found all across the universe, in the shape of our ears, of flowers and pine cones, the curve of an egg, the measurements of our arms and legs, the whorls of a snail's shell, the swirl of a hurricane seen from space, the lines of a spiral galaxy. They link space and nature and us.

When we get to use the computers to look up Leonardo da Vinci I google *the golden ratio*. A thousand images rush from the screen into my brain and there's a violin and an elephant's tusk and Sonic the Hedgehog and the Apple logo and the centre of a sunflower and a spiral galaxy. I run my finger along the lines on the screen and look at the pattern that repeats and echoes through the universe. I search for *spiral galaxies* and then I

feel like I've been lifted up and whirled into space. The swirl of the galaxy is dotted with stars that are salt-sprinkled into curves that spin into the blueblack ink of the infinite night sky. I print a picture and put it in my pocket where it nestles like a secret.

3   18   1   3   11   19

At break everyone gathers round me in the playground and I'm in the middle of red jumpers and
excited faces and I think *awesome* in my head in the
same way as Jamie said it. Everyone likes the blue
of my arm and the blue of the bruise
creeping down from under my hair.
They rub the roughness of my
cast and ask me if it hurts. I
shake my head no but I do tell
them about the crunchcrack when it
broke and that's their best bit. *Can we sign it*
can we sign it can we sign it Noah chants and he's
already holding a fat black pen like a sword ready to
fight to mark me first. So Year Six draws cats and

faces and *Minecraft* pigs and creepers and tries out graffiti writing and my cast is a blue blur of art. I push back my hair so everyone can see my glued-up head and Ahmed says will it scar and I nod like it's no big deal but inside I'm a blazing bright firework and the crowd goes *ooo*.

How'd it happen says Sam and I want to tell a story that's not about shouting and kitchen chairs and is about a wildboy and a swinging vine but before I can Noah says *it was probably his weirdo brother* and *he's a loony from the loony bin* and *have you seen his buggy*. Noah uses the word the boys in the park used and then another one that's different but the same really and then he says Max should be sent away to a madhouse. Then he pulls a face that's dribbly and his eyes criss-cross and his cheeks are puffed like a baby baboon and he looks nothing like Max but I know that's who he's being.

And my head is buzzing just like my arm did and fizzy shots of raging light are bouncing and spinning through my brain and I am red-hot liquid with a boy's

107

skin on top and it's bubbling and soon it'll start pouring from my eyes and ears and mouth and I'll be a puddle of sparks and lava. Sam is watching me and Noah is still laughing at his own stupid clever face and I haven't said anything at all because if I open my hot mouth then the liquid will pour out and I'll be gone.

The red jumpers are trickling back into other corners of the playground to play football and skipping rope and Bulldog. Then Ahmed says *shut up Noah* and Jamie says *yeah, don't be like that, mate* and Sam shoves Noah on the shoulder harder than friends shove each other even in football and Noah says the same sweary thing Dad said to a man from a church when they offered to cure Max with special prayers. He calls Max all the words he shouldn't and he remembers the big pushchair and the stupid book and the noises Max makes and the flap-bounce-bop rhythm of his walk.

And Jamie and Ahmed and Sam clench their fists in tight knuckled circles and they fight for Max and they swipe and kick and roar against Noah and puffed-cheek faces and awful names and words that make Mum cry and I'm still standing with one arm leadheavy with cracked bones and then the rest of me is cracked too and I can hear it happening inside me louder than my jigsaw arm snapping and louder than what is right beside me. I walk away with my mouth clamped closed but the hot seeps out from my cracks anyway and I can feel lava tears on my cheeks but I've said nothing at all.

5 **13** **16**

20

25

Ahmed and Sam and Jamie walk with me
when the home bell goes and they're full of
fight and excited words even though they've
all got detentions tomorrow and Mrs Havering is fiery
furious. She said *what is the* meaning *of this,*
boys? and I knew the answer but not the answer
she meant. No one said anything about Noah
and Max because we won't grass so Mrs Havering put
all the fighters on a list for litter-picking
tomorrow lunchtime. I wasn't fighting so I
don't have to stab Coke cans with a metal stick
and chase fluttering packets of crisps already
picked up by the wind.

Ahmed and Jamie and Sam tell me they

won't have Noah on their teams in PE football or playground football ever again and that he's out of order and they'll tear him up into little pieces and I am already in a thousand million black flecks but I want them to do it to me instead. I don't say anything because I didn't before and I can't unlock my mouth now and I feel so empty except for a burning ball of something that pulses in my tummy. Ahmed and Jamie and Sam think I am silent and sad and furious and they are right but they are wrong too because it's not for Noah and it's not even for Max. It's for me.

We go to the Wilderness after Sam goes home and Ahmed and Jamie shout into the sky but the trees feel like they're pressing in on me and I can't join in. I don't feel wild today and I don't write a 6 in the dirt.

I drag my feet into the house. Mum says hello and I nod and then she says Max had a wonderful day at school and that we should be proud and she's bursting with that fat happy balloon I had inside me yesterday that floated out of the window today and away maybe forever. She wants to celebrate but we can't go out and she can't cook Max's favourite dinner because he always has the same so she says she'll buy Max a little something and she'll make me cottage pie which is my favourite. I shake my head no and I want to run as far away as my skinny stick legs can spring me.

Max is with Angelique because it's a Tuesday and she says *hello Frank you look like you've been in the wars* and I nod yes but I don't say it. *Cat got your tongue?* asks Angelique and offers me thumbs up or thumbs down pictures and she laughs nicely but I don't take them because it's a joke.

Max is tipping a tube of sparkly water back and forth back and forth very close to his face but he is listening and he gets up in a scrabbling little bunny hop and he holds out the tube to me. I reach out for it and then Max jumps like he's just remembered something important and he has because he gives me a little picture of the sparkly tube and then holds out his hand. Angelique is suddenly smiling and she says *he's got it, I think he's got it that boy*. I give Max the card and he makes a song with no words and passes the toy. I take it and I can see the glitter swirling like a starry storm and Max is still watching it and he still wants it so I give it back when he hands me the card and I say *thank you* with my hands like Angelique does and then I go to my bedroom and I don't come out for cottage pie and I can't make any codes and I can't make sense of anything at all. I can hear Angelique telling Mum about Max using the cards and the pride in Mum's voice makes the air around me shimmer.

Mum puts her head round my door because I haven't come down for tea and she asks me if I'm poorly and I nod yes because I feel sick right down in the pit of my tummy where that ball of shame burns.

2 18 15

20

8

5 18

It used to be different before Mum
and Dad had Max. I didn't have the same
swooping tummy anxiety and knotty worry
and burning shame before he arrived.

I was five and he was hours, minutes and seconds
when they brought him home from the hospital. He
gave me a present and it was a red plastic motorbike
that I'd wanted for ever and ever. It was nestled in his
lap but it wasn't really from him and Mum and Dad
said *say hello to your little brother* and I wanted the
motorbike so badly that I could feel it in my hand
already but I didn't want to talk to the fat red baby
sitting in a car seat, because he couldn't
understand and he didn't feel like my

114

brother one tiny bit. Mum told me that he'd change, that he'd get bigger and be my biggest fan and we could share games and toys and secrets together.

But when I was eight and Max was three he wasn't sharing my games or toys or secrets and he wasn't being a little boy like they thought he would be. We were in our living room and I was watching quiet TV and Max was on his hands and knees rocking backwards and forwards and looking at his *Baby's Catalogue* and humming and not looking at any of us. Mum put her head in her hands and cried and cried and cried because she'd had a piece of paper from the doctor that they'd been on a special trip to see and she hated what it said about Max even though the doctor had said it at the appointment but this *made it official*.

She said to Dad *we wanted him so much we tried so hard for him and he's so far away*. Dad's voice was strange and tough and sad but he said *well we still want him and he's here and he'll keep getting closer and closer*. And he read the piece of paper and he said a very rude word and he said *Max is ours and he is*

Max and he's just as brilliant as any little boy. All his words wobbled a bit. Then he ripped up the piece of paper just like Max likes to do and Max came running over on his chubby baby legs to join in and then we all ripped up the doctor's letter into a million billion little pieces and Max was still just the way he'd always been.

I never read the letter before it became snow and dust but Mum sat me down and talked to me about it. She said Max was *autistic* and the word didn't mean anything to me so it hung between us empty in the air. Mum said it means Max sees and feels the world differently to me and to her and to Dad and to Jamie and to Ahmed and to Granny M and it's like he's wearing different glasses that filter things like sounds and light and colour so they stream into his brain in a way we don't understand. And all I could think about was *The Wizard of Oz* and the Emerald City and taking off the greenglass glasses to see that everything was different colours after all and was Max in Oz or was I? Mum said *it means he might need*

116

extra help with some things but he'll be good at other things too just maybe in a different way and she kept saying *different* as if it was almost the same. Mum stroked my cheek and said *he might not understand the way the world works sometimes.*

I looked at Max slapping the floor with his hand and giggling and I thought about being different and the way grown-ups speak and I said *I don't understand the world either.* Mum smiled a tired smile with only her mouth and said *me too, Frank, me too.* And then she held me tight and she said Max was my brother and how I might have to be brave for him sometimes. Then she asked me what Max and I were and I chanted back that we weren't just her world but we were her universe and her space and her stars and her sky and her galaxy and her cosmos too and she didn't let go.

21 14 9 22 5 18 19 5

The next day at school I feel sick every time I see Noah and every time I think about what he said and what I didn't say. I don't play football at lunchtime because of my arm anyway and I'm meant to be the referee but I mutter something about a headache and I know Ahmed doesn't believe me but he sits with me on the sidelines and shares secret sweets from his pockets.

When I get in I don't say anything to Mum even when she asks me questions and the main one is *Are you all right?* over and over. I watch rubbish TV that's so rubbish I fall asleep and when I wake up in a hot warm tangle of blankets and heat I hear scratchy scribble noises in the hall and it's not Max because he's on the floor in front of me drawing on a piece of paper that's almost as big as him. Then Mum comes in and she's with Mark and he's got his dog Neil with him. Neil's got the best feathery fan tail that thumps from side to side which means he's happy. I stroke his velvet ears. I think that Mum and Mark will have a cup of tea and talk about art like they always do but Mum says *Mark wants to know if you'd like to go for a walk with Neil.* I know that Mark doesn't want to know that but Mum has asked him to want to know that.

But I don't mind because I want to walk Neil and for him to be my wolf companion like a real wildboy would have and so still don't talk but I nod and put on my shoes and we walk to the park. I have a jolty flood of worry that the football boys will be there but they're not. Mark lets me hold Neil's lead which is midnight

blue. I wrap it round my hand and Neil pulls so it tightens against my skin but he doesn't pull so much that it hurts. Mark talks so I don't have to and he tells me about his job which is a designer and he explains it to me but I still don't really know what he does but I listen while he talks about galleries and prints but I don't say anything. Not one single word or syllable or letter.

Mark calls Neil *a gentle giant* and says that means he's as big as a horse but he wouldn't hurt a fly. I say *I didn't think horses hurt flies anyway* and then I realise I've said it from my mouth and not just mumbled it or said it in my head and it only took a stupid joke and a huge dog and how ridiculous is that.

I feel better now I've opened my mouth and spoken but I don't feel better about Noah and the fight at all. I scuff my stupid trainers that don't have ticks or high tops or coloured laces and I dig the toes into a heap of leaves. Mark looks at me and I know he can tell that there are words triptrapping their way up through my throat and just about to jump from my mouth and so I let them.

We talk about everything and something and nothing at all. When we are silent it is calm and my voice isn't shouting inside. When we do talk I tell Mark about football and school and the golden ratio code and the whole universe and then suddenly I tell him about Noah and the fight that I didn't fight. I feel lighter when the words are out and the deep seeping shame inside me doesn't go away but its colour fades a little bit. Mark doesn't say anything until he says *I've got a Max*. And he tells me he's got a brother called Stephen who is the same as Max but forty-two and different in a lot of other ways but Stephen likes spinning and hates noises but not all noises and he goes out on trips with a group of other grown-ups and he likes museums and bowling and the cinema when they turn the volume down and the lights up.

Mark shows me a picture on his phone and Stephen is looking sideways and showing his teeth but not smiling just like Max does when someone says *smile* but he isn't happy. He is all skinny angles and his hands are by his sides and I know they are frozen mid-flap. I ask where Stephen lives. Mark says Stephen lives in a house with lots of other people who need extra help but he goes to Mark's mum and dad every weekend and once a month Mark drives hundreds of miles all the way to Yorkshire to take Stephen for a pizza. Stephen doesn't come to Mark's house because he wouldn't like the change or the journey or the pizzas. I think about Max in a house he doesn't know and people who don't know to put Quavers on his plate and who turn the TV up to 21 when it can only be on 20 when Max is in a good mood and 12 when he's not.

I think about Max being hundreds of miles away, just a speck in the distance far away from me and I feel a prickle of something in my stomach. And then I think about living just me and Max and him banging his head on the floor and screaming and Mum not being there to find an emergency bubble tube and a cushion and to put a cool hand on his forehead and say *finished*

       finished

           finished

look at these bubbles Maxy and my tummy feels even stranger.

6

1 13

9 12 25

I go back to school the next day and I don't look at Noah at all. Mrs Havering stands at the front of the classroom and draws herself up to her full height. She stretches her spine upwards until she seems almost like a giant and I know she's going to say something important. She turns and writes something on the board and when she steps backwards I can read the words FAMILY TREE printed in her neat script. Mrs Havering pulls the corner of her shirt collar so that it's perfectly pointed and then she tells us about the Big Year Six Project. She asks Kai what a family tree is and he jokes that it's a tree that you have in your garden that belongs to your family and Noah sniggers even though it's a rubbish joke. Every time I hear his voice I feel a hot burning anger that bubbles with my own shame at not saying a word when he was saying all his terrible ones.

Mrs Havering says *that's not quite right* and then Jamie says *it's your family history*. Mrs Havering smiles a real smile and says *that's exactly right*. She draws a tree with quick strokes of her pen on the whiteboard and it's only a few swipes of ink but Mrs Havering is a good drawer. Then she writes the names ALEXANDER MARSHALL and MARYA PETROVA at the top and draws a line between them and lines down falling from them towards the branches. She says *these are my great-grandparents* and then she puts little crosses by their names and explains that this symbol means they're dead. It seems such a tiny little mark for something so big.

As she sketches, the tree fills up with names and

dates that spread across its leaves and drop down its leaves until she's made a map of her history. All the branches cascade from those two top names, her great-grandparents. There's a horizontal line between two people who got married and then vertical lines drop from them to show their children. If the children get married they get a horizontal line to connect them to that new person, and vertical lines for children.

As she draws she talks about each name and the person behind it. Her grandfather was an engineer on the railways and his mother, Marya, came from Russia a hundred years ago or more. Her sister is a doctor who lives in Australia. Her brother is a writer and he lives in Sussex and has three children *here they are on the branch below, Molly, Harriet and Zach.* Mrs Havering has a husband called Richard and a grown-up son called Laurie and he's got a baby on the way so Mrs Havering draws a little twig down from Laurie and his wife's branch but the baby isn't born yet so she doesn't write a name. When she shades the leaves on Laurie's branch, the one dipped down from her and her husband's names, she pauses in the blank space next to his name just for a flicker of a moment. She opens her mouth and then closes it again without saying a word.

Noah is sniggering again because Mrs Havering has written her real first name on the tree and it's Agnes, but everyone else is mesmerised by the quick flicks of her pen and the history emerging from the branches.

Mrs Havering tells us that our Big Project this year will be to make trees of our own families. She tells us we'll have to research our families and ask our parents and grandparents, and even great-grandparents if anyone has any, all about our family histories. She says we have to write biographies with as much information as we can possibly find out about each of our family members, including parents and siblings. She smiles and says we might find out new and exciting things about people we thought we knew well and that we should find photographs or draw pictures too.

Ahmed rolls his eyes and mutters something darkly about having too many relatives to fit even on an oak tree. His house is always full of cousins and second cousins and third cousins and aunts and uncles and grandparents and it definitely seems like he'll have more work to do than me because I only have Max and Mum and Dad and Granny M and Mum's brother and Dad's brother Simon and their parents but we never see them because they're a million miles away in Scotland where Dad grew up. We used to go up but Max doesn't like being away from home and now they're too old to come and see us. Mum's brother lives in America which is so cool but we never get to see him because it's even further than Scotland and he says he only comes back for weddings and funerals. I don't know how to write about our family and the history of Max and I don't want Noah to read his life and use those awful words.

Mrs Havering gives us new notebooks which have lined pages and blank pages and bright red covers. She says we have to record our research in them and that we'll build a Family Forest at the end of the Easter term. The Big Year Six Project isn't the same every year because last year they had chicks that they hatched from eggs and made scientific notes about their development and now they live in a coop in the caretaker's garden, and I'm secretly disappointed we're not doing that too. I like to go and see them scratching at the dirt and clucking softy to each other and sometimes the caretaker gives out eggs at home time and their yolks are like suns. I remember when I was in Year Two that the Year Sixes did family trees because they made great big trees from cardboard and tissue paper and paint and then made the Family Forest in the hall and we all walked through it.

2

5 6 15

18 5

When I get home I take out the
bright notebook and leaf through its
blank pages. Dad's parents and his
brother Simon are too far away to inter-
view properly and my tummy feels knotty
when I think about doing it over the phone
because I don't really know them at all. I
write their names down anyway because I
have to fill in that side of the tree even if it's
nothing more than names scribbled on a branch.
I only have Mum, Dad, Max and Granny M to ask
in person and I can't even ask Max because he's
still working on handing over the right piece of fruit
when Angelique shows him a picture.

I ask Mum about her life story and she seems a little surprised. She laughs and says that I know she was an artist and that she still is, she supposes. Her hands flutter to the bright silk of her headscarf as she talks. I start writing and let her voice scribble itself on to the pages of my notebook.

She grew up right near here with Granny M and Grandpa and he died when I was three. *He never got to meet Max* she says thoughtfully. She met Dad at university when they were both still teenagers and young and carefree. When he got his first job they went on a trip to Venice to celebrate, just packed up and drove to the airport and spent the whole weekend eating pasta and sailing up and down canals in special long boats called gondolas. She saw lots of the famous art there and when she came home she painted the first painting that she ever sold. She painted the universe in

ways people
had never seen it
before, microcosms
of dust particles and spin-
ning lights tracking across an infinite
space reduced on to a canvas. *Spiral galaxies*, I think
suddenly, and Mum keeps talking while that thought
bubbles in my head.

More and more people asked for her art, more
people than she could possibly paint for and she and
Dad bought a house with a studio in the roof and
then I came along and when I was a tiny baby she
would put me in a bouncing chair and paint the
universe again but it looked very different to her now
I was in it. And then Max came along and he wouldn't
sit in that bouncing chair without screaming and
screaming so she put down her paintbrushes and she
has been meaning to pick them up again for the
longest time and then her voice trails off and she says
very quietly *I'm just too tired and busy now, Frank.*

And in that moment I hate Max.

19 20 1 18 4 21 19 20

Mark comes round that evening to ask if I'd like
to go for a walk with him and Neil. He has a cup
of tea with Mum first and then chats to Dad
when he gets home from work and I'm impa-
tiently hopping from foot to foot waiting for
them to finish while Max tries to stick his
finger in Neil's ear and I catch his wrist
to stop him and he shrieks.

When we get outside, I ask Mark
about spiral galaxies because I can't
understand them and I think
that he's a grown-up so maybe
he might even though I know
by now that grown-ups just

pretend to understand a lot of the time. He runs his hand through his hair and throws a tennis ball for Neil who immediately tries to swallow it whole. Mark gets out his phone and types for a few moments and I see the same pictures that I looked at popping up on the screen. *Still interested in the code of the universe then*, he asks. I nod.

Mmm he says. *Well spiral galaxies follow the golden ratio proportions. I think they've got a flat disc of stars in the middle and arms full of stars that look like the spirals you can see in those pictures.*

I look at him and he pulls the tennis ball out of Neil's slobbery mouth and throws it again even though Neil is much more interested in eating the ball than chasing it.

The arms full of stars look brighter because they're bigger and younger than the stars in the middle. There are a couple of ideas that try to explain why spiral galaxies fit the golden ratio, but I don't know if we'll ever really know in our lifetimes. I like the mystery, don't you?

I shrug because I like knowing the answers to things even if I don't understand every little bit of it. Mark throws Neil's ball into the light that's melting slowly from the sky. *You know what's really cool* he says and I don't think anything could be cooler than spiral galaxies but I shake my head and say *what, what's cool?*

We're all made of stardust. Our bodies are made from the remains of stars and huge explosions in our galaxies. Everything in our bodies began with a huge bang in space billions of years ago. It's true, promise. Stars are born and they die, just like us. And when they die, they throw off the stuff they're made of and it works its way through space and into us. Everything in us first came from space. That's pretty cool, isn't it?

We're made of stardust.

It's the coolest thing in the universe.

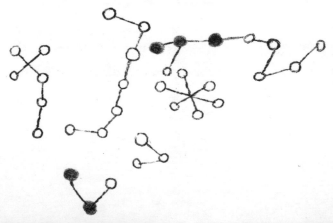

6 12 25 9 14 7

Ahmed and Jamie and I make a rope swing in the
Wilderness. We find loops and loops of twisted
blue rope in Jamie's garage and we borrow it to tie to
the thickest and highest branch of a tree. Ahmed
ties fat knots along it so that we can hold
tight on and wrap our legs around the
rope like monkeyboys and not
slip and slide off into the air.
My arm is still wrapped up tight in
itchy plaster that's grey and crumbling at
the edges and for a moment I'm worried my
bones will crack again but I can still curl my arms
around the rope and I soar through the air like a bird.
I feel feather tips nudging underneath my skin

waiting to burst through because I'm an eagle and a kite and a hawk and I swoop through the mud-tinged air looking for prey. I'm an astronaut, weightless in space. I am high above the world that holds Noah and his words that snag like thorns and away from Max's special things and meltdowns and screams. We swing until the sun has melted away and our cheeks are whipped red by the wind as we fly and I can almost stretch out my fingers and touch the stars that made us.

Afterwards we write **6** and **1** and **10** in the dirt just like always.

6

9

24

5

4

My cast is cut from my arm just as it began
to be a part of me. It is stained and crumbling
and a work of Wolverton art. Noah's name
shines N O A H and I can feel the letters have dripped
through into me and I can't cut them off and
get rid of the way he made me feel and the
way he made me act. He made the sick-sorry
feeling that began when I laughed at Max in the park
start to spread into my bones and wrap
around them like tentacles and they tighten
whenever I see him at school.

It's a Tuesday and Mum and I go to the
same hospital straight after school, but I don't
see Sadie or Mick or the Pritt Stick doctor

even though I look out for them specially. This doctor isn't funny like the other one and she doesn't tell me stories like Mick did but she has a buzzy round saw that looks like it's from a toolbox and not from a hospital at all. I am worried that I am in the wrong nightmare place and this doctor will cut off my arm and all the wormy shame that sits hot and heavy in my tummy and fills my blood will come pouring out covering the floor with rotten flesh and crawling insects and she will cackle and say she's curing me from being a monster.

Then I blink and the real doctor outside of my head says the saw won't cut my skin so don't worry but that my arm will feel like it's made of nothing and full of air when the blue wrapping is gone. I'm nervous and shaky scared when the buzzing starts but she's right because the saw doesn't touch my skin and my arm floats up on its own when the cast falls away and we all laugh.

My arm is puckered like after a too-long bath except it doesn't smell like I've had a bath. I wiggle my fingers and stretch and my arm is still too light and bloodless. I look at the distance from the tips of my fingers to my grubby wrist and then to my black-stained elbow and I think about how my arm is made from stars and magic measurements that make me fit into the code of the universe.

Mum says my arm needs a good wash and she looks at my strange skin and makes a face. Then she takes my dirty plaster-streaked hand and I think maybe now I'm too big to hold hands but I like the smooth warmth and so I curl my fingers around hers and then we swerve right and right into McDonald's and I don't have two Big Macs but I have one and a chocolate-sprinkled iced doughnut which tastes like the air at a fairground.

Because it's a Tuesday Max has his session with Angelique. Dad meets us at the door because he's left work early to be with Max like he promised Mum he would. He looks at my arm and pretends to be all shocked when he sees my newly naked arm and Mum and I roll our eyes at him.

My arm still feels zombieish and Angelique wants

to show me what Max can do and I have spellings to learn and *Minecraft* to play and Ahmed wants me to have a game of football in the park before it gets dark so I don't want to look at Max scrambling on the floor with his cards. But Angelique is smiling like she thinks of course I'd want to see this so I say *of course.* I sit on the floor where Max is curled around his *Baby's Catalogue* with his thumb running up and down the closed pages so they give a paper whisper. He has a purple mark in the dark hollow of his eye and I reach out slowly to wipe it away but it's a stained perfect circle of his own bony knuckle and I know that he has screamed and tried to hit and hit and hit the buzzing wasps out of his head.

I say *Max have you got something new to show me?* and I point to Angelique and Max looks at my hand and takes it in his and weighs it without its cast. Angelique kneels down and speaks with her hands and mouth and says *let's show your brother, eh.* She has three toys on the kitchen table but they're actually plastic fruit which isn't very fun. And she

143

says *Max show me the banana* and Max sideways looks at the fruit and he ignores the pear and the apple and he gives Angelique the banana. And I say *Max give me the apple* and he looks again and puts the apple in my hand and Dad is watching and says *that boy knows his apples*. There's a beat of silence when there should be laughter and Dad rolls his eyes and says he's *wasted on us* but he gives Max a gentle high five and Max shows us he knows what a pear is too and then we dance to a pocket full of posies and we all fall down.

Mum goes to bed early that night because she says she's very tired from our trip out and Dad puts Max to bed and I don't think Mum can possibly sleep through all the shrieks but she doesn't get up.

4

15

7

Mark comes to the house after school the day after my blue cast is gone. He sees it not being there straightaway and gives me the thumbs up. He has a cup of tea with Mum and Max except Max has Quavers instead and I play with Neil in the living room and he gives me his paw and rolls over and begs and I try to teach him to bark numbers but he doesn't get it yet.

I want to teach him to do sums because I saw a YouTube video where a man shouted things like seven plus five and his dog would pause for a moment like it was thinking and then bark back twelve times. Dad says the dog isn't really counting but I don't care if he thinks that. I keep trying to teach Neil to bark on command so we can start on numbers but it's really difficult because I don't know how to make him bark. He sniffs where the cast is missing and I think he can smell the stain that Noah has left inside me. But he rubs his wiry muzzle against my hip and then Mark comes into the room holding Neil's lead and his orange rubber ball and says *let's take Max with us* and I say *what?*

Mum has to come too but she walks behind like she's always that slow. She's pale and it looks like she's pulling her legs through mud but she's smiling in a way I don't remember. Max has his giddy-up reins on so Mark walks him and I walk Neil. I am furious and I don't look at Mark because he was mine and he's ruined everything. Mark talks to Max like he'll answer and says things like *how's school, mate* and *what's the best thing there* and *can you see that sparrow over there* and he tells Max about seeing a heron last week. I don't talk to anyone and not even Neil. I don't want to share Mark and Neil with Max. Max is bouncing along in his reins and he claps and whoops and his fingers aren't in his ears and he's flapping up high.

Max likes Neil and he wants to touch him and so Mark shows him how to stroke his ears and pat his head softly softly. Neil does a grumbly sigh which means he's happy and that he wants his ears scratched. Max's fingers dance in Neil's fur and then he reaches out his hands and he says *dog* with them and Mum beams and beams and she puts her hands up to her face to feel her own happiness on there. *That's right*, I say, *dog. Well done*. And I say it like I don't mean it but I think I do because that's Max's first word.

Max wants to hold Neil's lead and so I let him and Max holds Neil and Mark holds Max. There's a chain of man and boy and dog and they stumble along unbroken and Max is making his noises louder than when he goes on the swings and there are big boys and girls and little boys and girls in the park and some of them are from school and suddenly I don't care and I say it again *well done Max, well done*.

Mum calls Dad to tell him about Max's word and then she calls Angelique and Granny M and her brother Dan and her best friend Hazel and her other best friend Natalie. She cries when she's on the phone and she catches my eye and smiles with her whole face and my heartbeat skips because I really can't remember her face looking quite like that for a long time. She's talking really fast and saying how they should all meet up for drinks *soon because it's just been too long, hasn't it?* She still looks tired and china pale but she looks happy. Angelique is so happy that she cries on the phone too and then she says she's going to tell her mum in France.

Dad makes whooping whoop noises when he gets in and ruffles Max's black curls which he instantly hates and we're back to fingers in ears and a stiff little body screaming on the carpet. But Mum and Dad don't seem to mind and when Max bangs his head on the floor to stop the explosions inside his brain they put a cushion under him and they are still smiling. Then Dad calls his brother Simon and his best friend

Steve and his parents far away in their map crease of Scotland where it's cold even when it's not winter and they have to wear hats in bed. And news of Max's dog word is seeping out and out and away into all of the corners of the world and I feel proud but I just keep the feeling inside and don't say a word.

After all the phone calls are finished, Mum clasps her hands together in joy and Dad opens a bottle of champagne just like he used to do when Mum sold a painting in a gallery. He pops the cork oh-so quietly so it doesn't upset Max because it's Max we're cele-brating this time. Dad pours the fizzing honey liquid into the tall glasses that I remember from forever ago and he raises a toast to Max. Max doesn't look up from the kitchen table where he's drawing with a look of concentration on his little face, brand-new pencils from the art shop in town clutched in his fist. They were a special present for his word and Dad bought them on his way home and when Max saw them he stopped banging his head and reached out his hands for them. He's drawing Neil the dog and I can see the gentle spikes and tufts of his fur emerging on the paper.

I try a sip of the champagne but it's as horrible as I remember and it burns sourly on my tongue. Mum and Dad lean in close together and whisper softly while I watch Max make a portrait of his friend. Mum is leaning against the counter and then suddenly she slips out of view and down down down to the ground and her limbs aren't her own any more and there's a tinkling crunch of broken glass as her champagne pools on the floor beside her. She's making an awful noise and her muscles are twitching and jerking and her face doesn't look like hers any more.

Dad kneels on the floor to try to stop Mum's scarf-wrapped head banging into the kitchen cabinets and his hands are sticky with blood from catching them on the champagne soaked splinters that fan outwards from Mum's body. And in a voice I haven't heard before he shouts *call an ambulance and tell them your mother's having a seizure, tell them our address, tell them to come quickly.*

My fingers are shaking and I nearly can't make them work properly. When the line clicks on at the other end I tell them in a voice made of something very cold that *my mum is having a seizure and can they come quickly please?* Then Dad takes the phone from me and his blood drops and fizzes from his hands into the flood of champagne.

The ambulance arrives in a frenzy of bright blue lights that wash the kitchen walls and make Max scream. The paramedics dance around Mum's twitching body and the champagne smell rises around us. I can see the silver flash of a needle dipping into the bright blue vein of her trembling hand and then Granny M arrives and she takes us away from the noises and glass and low urgent voices.

After Mum and Dad are whisked off to the hospital in the back of the ambulance Granny M goes to sweep up the glass and clean up the blood before Max can hurt himself. I am trying to breathe and it doesn't feel right. I gasp in lungfuls of air and none of them are going to the right place and I am dizzy and sick. I keep picturing Mum laughing with her head bent close to Dad's and then the sudden sick shock split second when she slipped down and the moment broke. I can't sit still and I stand up and shake my arms and legs and I pace up and down and Granny M comes in and puts the TV on and then turns it off again because none of us knows what's going on. She kisses the top of my head and she says that it'll *all be OK* but we both know she doesn't know that. She calls Dad a few times and finally he picks up and says that Mum's *stable* and my lungs and the air start working together again.

Granny M doesn't give Max a bath because it's not worth it and instead she cuddles him close while she gently tugs off his clothes and lifts him into his pyjamas. Max sucks his fingers urgently and he looks around for Mum but he doesn't melt but he won't go to sleep either and neither will I. We all sit on the sofa huddled together and after a while I am dragged into a fitful sleep until I hear the click of the front door and see Dad helping Mum up the stairs.

The next day Granny M gets me up at the normal time even though I feel like my eyes are full of sand and I haven't slept at all. At breakfast Dad isn't wearing his work clothes and he sits opposite me and tells me that Mum had a seizure and that if it ever happens again I have to call 999 just like I did so well last night and tell them what's happening and give them our address in a really clear voice. He pauses to clear his throat because his own voice suddenly isn't very clear and then he tells me that Mum is *going to be OK* and *they don't think it'll happen again* because the doctors have given Mum some medicine to take every day. It might make her a bit sleepy and so we all have to be good and we all have to help her as much as possible. Max is sitting right next to me quietly sucking Quavers into a mush but Dad isn't even looking at him, he's looking at me.

19 3 18 5 1 13

9

14

7

At school I fall asleep at my desk and Mrs
Havering wakes me with her cool gentle hand
on mine. The doctor comes to see Mum at
home that evening and he gives her more
pills and she swims up from sleep just long
enough to smile at me when I creep into
her room before bedtime. One of her
hands is bandaged where she cut it on
the champagne glass and there's a
bruise on the back of her other
hand where the hospital had
to put more needles into
her to stop the
seizure. And I

155

don't know what's wrong with her and no one will tell
me even when I ask over and over and Dad will only
say **_she's going to be fine_**. I just want to

scream
and scream
and scream

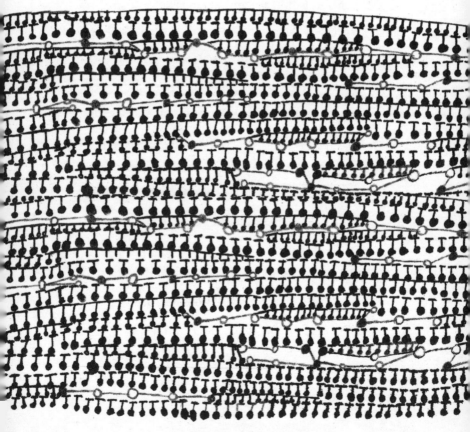

into space until my voice

bounces

off

a   galaxy

and

shatters

the

sky.

1
6
18 1 9 4

Two days later Mum is
better because she's up
and about and baking and
laughing and making me eat
peas and opening bags of
Quavers for Max and making
sure we've got everything we need
for school on Monday and helping
us with our homework. Her eyes are
very bright and when I ask her whether
she knew that a day on Jupiter only lasts
for nine hours and fifty-six minutes she
takes a very long time to answer and I think
she's forgotten what I said.

Mum has been climbing the stairs to the rickety attic room and she says she's clearing it out so she can maybe even start painting again now Max is at school. But for now it means I can't go up there when Max is shouting or when I want to write on the canvas the coded words of worry that are eating away my insides. I write them in tiny pencil print that can be erased with the swish of a rubber in the back of my bright red family tree notebook instead.

Max has not once been sent home from the spaceship school for being a hoppity handful of beans and now he is on full days. He doesn't get into trouble like I would for doing the kinds of things he does, like throwing chairs or not sitting down when he should or humming when the teacher is speaking. Mum says she is so happy with him and how hard he works. His green notebook with letters from his teachers say that he is brilliant and funny and wonderful and that he can find some alphabet letters on a board without any help. Max loves his teacher and he especially loves Rhoda. She wears her vest the right way round now and Max sometimes lets himself touch it but he pulls his hand away superfast to stop the bright yellow burning him and staining his skin.

Max hasn't said anything new since *dog* but he says it with his hands each time he sees Neil. We walk him with Mark and Mum comes too or sometimes Granny M when Mum is too tired and Max says *dog dog dog dog dog dog dog dog dog dog dog dog dog dog dog dog dog dog dog dog dog dog* for ever and ever until I think his hands must ache with tired and cold because he won't wear gloves but every word means he is happy.

I look at him speaking with his hands and I look at the smile that breaks his face in two when he sees Neil and I feel cold inside because all I can think about is Mum and her bright bruisey eyes and her bird bones and her falling down down down and I'm afraid. And I think that she wouldn't be so tired and so pale and so thin if it weren't for Max waking up and shouting and Max lashing out and melting and Max not being able to just be like other children.

Once Granny M comes with us even though Mum says she's not too tired but her feet are stumbly and Granny M holds Mum's hand just like she's a child all over again. She puts her head close to Mum's bird-boned face and I hear a whisper of what she says and it's that she has to tell us soon and I think *tell us what?*

4 1 18 11
14
5
19 19

Granny M is in the kitchen and she's started peeling potatoes for supper. Mum had another fit last week and she's too tired and fuzzy from the new drugs the doctors gave her to cook the supper today. I didn't see the seizure so I couldn't call 999 but I still feel sick and icy with fear when I remember her terrible tumbling body shaking on the kitchen tiles and I try to shake it out of my head. Granny M squeezes my shoulder and tells me to keep my chin up and haven't I got something to do that might take my mind off it all?

I go and get my bright red notebook because

it's full of snow-white pages except for Mum's story and the codes I can't scribble on the canvas upstairs. Mrs Havering gives us half an hour every Friday to write and research but I just twirl my pencil round the codes on the back pages because I don't want to write the story of Max. But today at break I could hear Noah shouting about how he'd found out that his great-grandfather had been a hero soldier in World War Two and Kai said his great-great-uncle had flown planes in the RAF against the Germans and my stomach lurched when I thought of the blank pages in my book.

I sit at the kitchen table and draw a tree on one of the unlined pages and I expect it to look a bit rubbish but I actually think it's quite good. I hold my pen tightly and swirl the nib over another page drawing spirals and squares before I ask Granny M to tell me her story starting at the beginning. When I do, she looks surprised just like Mum did and I don't think she's ever had someone ask her that question before. She takes off her cooking apron

163

and sits down next to me.

She tells me her parents were very poor. They were from up in the very north of the country and her father worked in the mines, deep below the earth in the darkness where he dug out coal and breathed in black air and stained his skin dark every day with the dust. He would come home with a cloud drifting up from his clothing and even when he scrubbed and scrubbed with soap and water the dust wouldn't shift and it was a part of his skin, a tattoo of his work. He would cough up great black chunks and Granny M would think that his whole lungs were coming up.

When Granny M was six and her sister was four, the mine that her father was working in exploded. The earth blew right out of the ground and the spray of black splattered across the town. Granny M was in school and she felt the ground boom beneath her feet and the teachers knew exactly what had happened. Their husbands and their brothers and their sons worked in that mine and they all ran out of the school building and raced towards the explosion. Some of the men were already staggering away but some of them were dead and some of them were trapped beneath the earth under the collapsing weight of the mine.

Granny M's father wasn't one of the dead but he could never work in a mine again. He was hoisted out by the men in the town and lay gasping on his back and coughing great clouds of blood-thickened black dust up from his lungs. He went to bed after that day and he didn't get up again. *I don't know if it was his body or his mind that gave up*, says Granny M. *I don't think it really mattered.*

She tells me that's enough for one day and then she helps me write the names of her father and mother and puts little crosses by their names to show that they're not alive any more. I put in the name of her sister, Sylvia, myself because we've been to visit her before. She has a thousand little glass paper-weights filled with bubbles of colour and I wanted to touch them more than anything but she wouldn't let children go near them. Mum held Max very tightly.

The next day we work on our projects at school.

Mrs Havering wants us to write up the stories we have so far and illustrate them if we can. *The books of your families* she says and she lets us all go to the IT room. We traipse along the corridors and some of the class get typing straightaway. The rest of us sit around the big table in the middle of the room and start to design the first of our books.

Mrs Havering has a pile of blank covers and a pile of lined sheets that we can staple inside the covers once we've copied the stories from our red notebooks. The books will hang from the branches of the trees when we make the Family Forest in the school hall. We're meant to have the story of a different family member in each one, even if it's just a page and some drawings. Mrs Havering tells us that *everyone has a story that's longer and more complex than we might ever imagine, even a tiny baby*. I write up Mum's story neatly and stick a photo of her and Dad on the cover and I've even got some pictures of her paintings that I printed at home so I can glue them to the inner pages to show that she's an artist.

Jamie sticks a photo of his mum to the cover of her story and tells us that she's a surgeon which is true and that she is a spy which definitely isn't. I get a new blank cover but I don't have a photo of my great-grandfather and I don't know what he looked like at all so I let my hand take over and when I look back at the picture I've made it's like I'm looking at me as a grown man. Jamie gives an impressed whistle and says my drawings are always the best in the class and this one looks almost real and I burn with pride.

$$8 \quad 9 \quad 19 \quad 20 \quad 15 \quad 18 \quad 25$$

Dad and I play some Hangman before school, except
I'm not going to school today. It's the last day before
October half-term and the whole of Year Six is going
on a trip to the Natural History Museum. It's
going to be so much better than doing
another comprehension, which is
what a Friday normally is.
Mum takes her pills
every morning and
evening, which she keeps in a
locked box just in case Max decides
he's going to eat colours today. Today she pops
out some different ones from a painkiller packet and
she's got a terrible headache. I feel sick in my tummy

because looking after us is making her poorly and I try to be as good as gold. Max didn't sleep last night, not one tiny little bit. He bounced and jumped and squealed and I pushed my head under my pillow and scrunched my fingers in my ears until his shouts were just a wash of noise like the sea. Dad puts his arm around Mum and says that the neighbours must hate us but Mum doesn't smile and one of our neighbours is Mark and he says he likes to hear the noises of a family but probably he doesn't think that at 3 a.m.

Mum rubs her face and says she's too tired to function, and her head is killing her. Dad says he'll come home early from work and take Max to the swings as soon as he gets in from school so that Mum can get some rest. This isn't the routine because Dad doesn't usually go to the park and Max won't like it and so I know Mum must feel really poorly. Right then, I hate Max in a fresh wave of anger. Mum puts her arms around me and I feel her jutting bird-bones and she kisses the top of my curls and tells me to be good and how she wishes she could come with me to the museum because it's like looking through a thousand layers of time and history all at once.

The wind is nibbling my ears and I've forgotten my hat and Year Six gets on an old smelly coach. We don't have to wear uniform and that makes everyone look strange and far away from usual. I am wearing my favourite bright yellow jumper and Jamie is wearing the same one because we bought them together last year. We planned it that way and we say we will be twins today and that no one will be able to tell us apart. Jamie is blond like pictures of angels and I'm not so we are definitely joking but Mrs Havering calls me Jamie for fun and I think that maybe the rumours about the cane in her desk aren't true. There are rows and rows of seats on the coach and so I sit with Ahmed and far away from Noah. Noah doesn't talk to us any more and he thinks this is a bad thing for us but it's not.

Ahmed has a new game on his phone and we swipe at zombies and I'm good at it. I beat his high score and he doesn't mind because he says he doesn't play it much anyway so I pow and blast them to brains and gunk until the coach belches up to the museum. We climb down its narrow chewing-gummed stairs and clamber up grey stone steps and take clipboards and worksheets and promise to meet the teachers at checkpoints every hour and then we scatter like birds.

This place is full of bones. My lightning-white bones in my cloudy X-ray are tiny splinters compared to the ancient skeletons of beasts from forever ago that have been puzzled back together and are rising around us. I feel like a minuscule dot in the whole huge history of the world. I want to touch the bones but they make my eyes feel dizzy and I think if I reach out a hand then I'll fall and so I look and look and look and this is the world a million years ago right here. I take the little scrap of spiral galaxy that I always keep in my pocket and that shows me the code that connects the universe. I can see it threading its pattern through history, through the bones and animals and plants that tower around my head. The measurements spin through the curls of ammonites and the winding fronds of fossilised ferns, the arced skulls of dinosaurs and the curve of unhatched eggs.

Ahmed and Jamie want to find stuffed animals and not just look at bones and at first I think they mean toys but these are real dead animals made to look alive. There are hundreds of them sealed into glass boxes as if they might escape. They stretch and roar and graze and pounce but they're stiff and glassy-eyed and some of them have dribbles of glue on the seams clutching their skin. I think they're disgusting but Jamie presses his face into the glass and smears it with his breath so he can look closer and closer at a snarling crocodile. Ahmed tells us that crocodiles have the strongest bite of any animal in the world and Jamie wants one as a pet so he can set it on people. I look at the crocodile and its green puckered armour and its blank eyes and I feel funny because it's dead and it's in a strange glass tank with pretend plants like it's in its real world but it doesn't look right at all. I feel sorry for that crocodile.

Ahmed reads a leaflet and tells us there's a room

with loads of butterflies but I don't want to see dead bugs pinned to the wall. Ahmed rolls his eyes and says *they're alive, dummy*. He shows me and Jamie the leaflet and there's a whole tunnel that looks like a tent filled with butterflies from all over the world. The pictures show bright wings nestled in stretched-out palms. I want to hold a butterfly. We find the tent tunnel which is difficult because it's outside and Jamie and Ahmed argue about which way it is and I get distracted by a stuffed wombat because I've never seen anything like it.

In the tent the air is full of butterflies and I never knew that they could have a smell but they do. It's musty and fresh at the same time and I like it. The air is thick with a warm heat and I roll up the sleeves of my jumper. There are big wooden troughs filled with flowers and plants and it's a lot better here than looking at the dead animals in their tanks. The butterfly keepers wander round and they say *oh don't touch them like that* and *they like this* and *they don't like that*. It still seems strange to be standing in a

173

plastic tunnel outside a museum in the middle of London with hundreds of butterflies whirling round like a velvet tornado but they have real plants and nestley places to hide. It's not their real world but I think it's getting there.

The butterflies land on me because I'm wearing bright yellow and they think I'm a flower and they do the same to Jamie. It's tickly and shivery when a butterfly walks up your arm. When one lands on my hand I look at its wings and I can see through all the colours that its wings are torn like tissue paper. When I move it flies up again and the ragged edges blur into a whirl of pattern and it swoop swooshes to another human flower.

There are lots of Wolverton children in the butterfly room and they cup butterflies in their palms and try to take pictures before they flit away again. I see Noah throwing himself in front of the butterflies as they hunt for flowers and nectar and try to hide themselves in the green fronds of plants. His hands snatch for them and they arch away from him and flap high

174

to the ceiling in a panic of wings. I want to tell him to stop and to leave them alone and that he has to let them do what they want or it's not fair. I don't say anything though and the butterflies don't land on him even though his top is bright orange. Noah swears and says *this place is rubbish and for babies* and he stomps out and more butterflies cloud upwards from the flowers. I reach out my hand and one lands on my fingertip. I grin and Ahmed takes a picture.

I bike home from school after I get off the coach back from the museum, letting the wind whip up my hair and shriek past my ears. Ahmed says he can smell when it's going to snow and that today smells like snow. Jamie said it wasn't even properly winter yet and it was too early for snow but Ahmed insisted.

The sky is dark and rippling with heavy grey clouds and I hope he's right because we could go sledging in the Wilderness like last year. Dad made my sledge for a Christmas present a few years ago, and it has a horn and special lights that cast an arc-beam of light that glitters the white snow. Last year we stayed out until my sledge's lamp was the only light left and the Wilderness was absorbed into inky blackness and then we went home and Mum made us all hot chocolate with whipped cream and marshmallows.

I let out a whoop as I fly down the hill on my bike, my scarf rippling behind me like an aeroplane's banner. It's properly half-term and I'm going round to Jamie's this evening to play on his new PlayStation which has a virtual reality headset which can send you anywhere in the world and I'm so excited that I don't really see what's in front of me until the lights are blinding.

8

1

3

15

19

Our street is in chaos. There is a
police car and an ambulance and their
blue lights collide in the air and throw
shapes into the shadows. For one moment I'm excited
because it looks like something on
television and then I'm scared because
this is real life and something has
happened. I look desperately for someone I know, for
anyone who could tell me what's
happening, but all the faces are strange
and the lights make them look ghostly.
I start to feel afraid because the car and
the ambulance aren't moving and
shrieking into another street with their

178

sirens calling out a warning. They're still and they're parked outside our ramshackle house.

I start to run up to the door but before I can open it with the key I have In Case of Emergencies I see that it's already ajar and so I start forward. Before I can go inside a huge arm presses across my chest and I'm swept off the doorstep and it feels like I'm underneath a crashing wave. I wriggle and try to get free because everything feels horribly wrong. I look up and my heart is thudding against the hand that's pushing me back.

Mark is looming above me and he says *come on Frank, step back, you can't go in there just yet.* I shout out why not why not and I start to fight harder against the hold he has me in and the harder I fight the stronger he gets so I start to be like Max and I spit and I bite and I scratch and for those moments I'm a wildboy bursting his bones and out of his skin.

Mark is saying something and the words drop into the air but I can't make them reach my ears because

179

of the roaring sound in my head. And then I see Dad running in a tangled sprint of limbs and he's wearing his suit straight from work and he looks wrong because Dad never runs in his suit and for a split second I want to laugh. His face is wrong too and I realise that he is crying. I've never seen him cry like this before, his whole face twisting with every sob. Not when Max is at his baddest and Mum is sobbing or when his granny died of very old age or when our ginger cat Pernikitty had to be put to sleep.

Dad is talking to one of the ambulance people and I can't hear what they're saying. I twist myself in knots trying to get free from Mark's iron arms and I see Rhoda in her bright jacket. I wonder why she isn't on the school bus but instead she's just holding Max's hand and Max is very quiet. There is something even more wrong with what I'm seeing but I can't fit the pieces together.

And then a question hits me and it tumbles in a shuddery rush from my mouth because I know what's wrong.

And then I ask them in a voice that screams its way out

WHERE'S MUM?

And then Dad opens his mouth but he can only speak in sobs and he is swept away by the police inside the gaping mouth of our house.

And then Mark is holding me by the shoulders and his fingers are pressing into my bones and he's saying something but I don't know what.

And then a woman in an ambulance uniform is saying something and she's pointing to me and to Max and I know we're not allowed to see what's going to happen. A radio clipped to her chest keeps making chirrupy crackles and Max jumps and I reach forward to hold his other hand.

And then a real-life police officer with numbers stitched across his shoulders comes forward and he says something to Mark and then it's just me and Max being herded away from our front door and Rhoda is standing with the ambulance lady with a hand clamped over her mouth. I look back and I cry out for Dad, and for Mum, and Mark tells me that Dad'll be with me soon but he doesn't say anything about Mum and Mum doesn't come running like she normally does.

And then we are in Mark's kitchen which is the same shape as ours but it is clean and white and all of the mugs match because they're all white too. Neil is there and Max twists his fingers into the dog's long grey fur and even though everything is new he is OK. I am not because no one is telling me anything and I can't get enough air. I press my face against the window so I can stare out on to our blue-drenched street but Mark gently leads me away and makes me a cup of tea with four sugars even though I don't drink tea and Mum doesn't like us having too much sugar because it'll rot our teeth right out of our heads. He puts CBeebies on for Max and he brings out a blanket and wraps him up tightly just like Max likes. Then Mark gets an iPad and quick as a flash he downloads games with shapes and games with colours and games with funny little creatures blobbing about on the screen. And Max sits on the sofa curled up with his cartoons and his games and Neil.

Mark gives me my tea in its perfect white cup and I sit at the table and my eyes feel hollow. I look at the brown liquid that's steaming and swirling from having to stir in all the teaspoons of teeth-rotting sugar and I can't stop staring until the whirlpool is calm. He tells me Mum suddenly wasn't very well at all and that Rhoda and Max came home on the bus and found her poorly and now all these people are here because of that. I know she's had another fit and I feel a bit better when I think that because she's always been all right after them. I ask if she's OK in a voice that tears like tissue paper.

And then Mark sets down his own white teacup and he looks at me and he tells me he doesn't know.

And then the world stops spinning.

And then all the chaos rushes in.

7 15 14 5

I am not the boy with the strange
brother any more. I am not the boy
who has magic footballing feet. I am not
the boy who can do maths faster than the speed
of light. I am not the boy who's a bit too skinny. I
am not the boy who didn't fight Noah. I am not the
boy who lives in a ramshackle house that spills over
with colour. I am not the boy who writes his feelings
and thoughts and memories in secret code. I am
not the boy who rides his bike too fast down
hills and whoops at all the people who
watch the whizzing blur fly by them.

I am the boy whose mother died.

5   3   8   15

Dad comes home from the hospital
and he says *she looked very peaceful* but
he says it in the way that people say
things because that's what everyone
has always said and so it sounds about
right. He puts his hands on my
shoulders like Mark had done and it
makes me feel like I have to be bigger
and braver than I could ever imagine
being. He tells me that Mum had been
ill, a tumour inside her head but that this
wasn't meant to happen, she was going to
be fine, it was going to be fine, they were
going to tell us when she was OK again.

She was having treatment every week at the hospital, all those slipped-out whispered visits in the summer when Granny M looked after us and she never said a word and I think of the haircut and the silk scarves that I thought were to stop Max's reaching fingers and I feel sick. *She said you boys had enough on your plates* he says and all his words have the trace of sob etched in every syllable. He keeps saying *she was going to be fine* over and over and over until the words don't sound like words any more and then Granny M takes my hand and gets me a Coke that I don't want while Dad rocks on his heels and cries.

Granny M strokes my cheek and tells me that *Mum's head started bleeding inside* and that *it was very quick* and that *no one could have known*. And I wish I'd known but at the same time I wish I hadn't and all I can imagine is a head full of blood, deep red swirling and crashing until there's nothing but darkness. Then Granny M says *no one could have known* again and again and everyone is stuck on repeat and I want to scream until it echoes too.

2 18 15

11 5 14

It's been four days since Mum died.

Dad hasn't gone to work or emptied our bins or cooked our dinners or even had a shower. His eyes have sunk into his skull and he looks like a skeleton with a field of grey-splashed stubble creeping across his jaw. He doesn't cry in front of us today but the skin around his eyes is red and raw and always damp as if he's just stopped or he might just start. When I come down for breakfast he sits at the kitchen table and he stares
into the space that we've all
fallen into and he
doesn't say a
word.

189

I get myself some Coco Pops and I get Max a packet of Quavers and make sure he sits at the table to eat them. Dad wears his tatty old dressing gown that Mum gave him a hundred years ago when they were still at university and Max and I were far away in the future. He hasn't even put clothes on when visitors come round and there have been a lot of visitors. Max hated it at first but now he just slinks down on the sofa like a worried cat and chews at the heel of his hand while the visitors put things like pasta bakes and stews in huge foil containers into our freezer. They make Dad tea and sweep away the undrunk cups that cover the table and wash them up and stack them neatly in a perfect pile next to the sink and then they think that must have made things better.

I put my bowl in the sink and I'm about to leave it there but I stop and wash it up because my bowl from yesterday is still there and the Weetabix crumbs have glued themselves to the spoon. I squeeze too much washing-up liquid and the sink fills with bubbles and the bowl slips from my hand and smashes. Dad looks up as if he's heard something from far away and then carries on staring into space. I pick up the bits of bowl and put them in the bin and then I sit on the sofa and I cry.

Granny M comes over in the evening and empties the bins and puts a pasta bake in the oven because we'd just forget about them otherwise. Max will only eat packets of Quavers anyway. He won't have a bath which isn't new but he isn't having any baths at all which is definitely new. Granny M tries to coax him and she tries to tell him he can have special treats after his bath but she doesn't have what Max wants and he goes to his special book and riffles through the pages until he finds the little plastic cards that have all our family's names and pictures on them and he hands Granny M the card that says *Mummy* and my heart cracks and I think hers does too.

At night-time, when it's time for his bed and his story and his sleep snuggles he stalks round the house looking for her and when he can't find her in the cupboard under the stairs or behind the curtains or in her bed then he opens his mouth and he howls. It comes deep from his belly and he's never made a sound like it before. It is a note of sadness that echoes through my bones and there's an ache inside me that feels like they're fracturing.

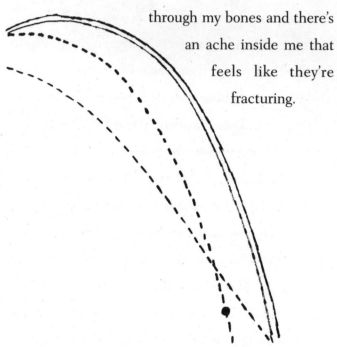

4

21

19   20

It's been six days since
Mum died but I had to
count because time feels
like it's fallen apart. It's the
day of her funeral but Max isn't
coming because it will be too
bright and too sad and too strange.
It is too bright and too sad and too
strange for me. I wear a brand-new
black suit that itches and that I will never
wear again. The funeral is full of people
saying it was *such a tragic loss* and she was *too
young* and *what a shock* and did we *need anything*
and all their words hum in the background.

Granny M takes me into the room where the funeral will happen so I can see the coffin. When I see it I feel my knees start to tremble and I have to hold Granny M's hand so hard that my knuckles turn white. I've never seen a coffin in real life before and it suddenly seems such a horrible idea to have a diamond-shaped box with a dead person inside it while all around it are the people they've left behind. I didn't see Mum after she died so I only have my imagination and it whirls and roars with images of her cold grey face stiff and lifeless. I put my hand on the smooth wood and I can't believe she's actually in there and I tap

dot-dot dot-d a s h-dot-dot d a s h-dot-d a s h-d a s h

And she'll never say it back.

Granny M cries all the way through the funeral because her daughter is dead and the tears cut crystal rivers down her cheeks but she doesn't make a sound. Dad cries too but he howls like Max and I don't do anything at all except stare at the wooden box and try not to imagine Mum in there. When the coffin disappears behind a curtain I reach out my hand and I can feel the crack opening up between us as she disappears forever to be turned back into stardust.

Afterwards we have tiny sandwiches in a room that smells like the gym at school. Angelique is here and Natalie and Hazel and they never got to have that night out that they promised after Max said *dog*. Dad's parents aren't here, tucked up far away in Scotland and in their sympathy card they said how sorry they were not to be able to make the journey and I was sad then but now I'm here I don't want anyone to be here at all.

Dad's brother Simon leads him round the room like a tiny child and they get further and further away from me and I stand all alone. Mum's brother Dan squeezes my shoulder and tells me I'm brave and I don't know what to say because I'm not brave. I'm barely breathing and my chest feels bruised whenever I try. Dan gives me a glass of squash and I can tell he's trying to find some more words to say but no one knows what to say to the poor motherless boy so he just squeezes my shoulder again and drifts away.

Mark sees me standing on my own frozen in space and pinned in place by the horror of it all and he wanders over but he doesn't talk either. It doesn't feel like he's desperately shaking his brain for the right words to fall out and he just sits with me while Dad zombie-walks from person to person and I don't feel so alone.

Some faces there feel familiar but I can't remember their names even after they come up and hug me and make my suit itch against me. Ahmed and Jamie are here with their parents and they're wearing suits too and it looks strange. They both give me hugs and it feels wrong because we never hug and I shrug them off and go and stand in the loos away from everything and everyone.

When I come back from the loos all people seem to do is chat and drink glasses of wine and some of them even laugh. I want to scream until my face is scarlet with rage and shout at them to stop and to remember that my mother is dead.

During the funeral Max stayed at home with Rhoda, who holds my hand between both of hers when we get home and then she pulls me into a fierce hug that knocks the tears out of me and I cry and cry and cry while she rocks me like a baby.

I know she'd been with Max when they'd gone into the too-quiet house when no one answered the door and she'd pushed the handle and found it unlocked like it nearly always was. She'd thought maybe Mum had forgotten the time and was out shopping even though that wasn't like her at all and then she saw a shape in the kitchen and she'd bundled Max back on to the bus even though that wasn't on his timetable and he screamed and thrashed and bit and then she went back in the house and rang 999 and the whole street exploded into sirens.

I know Rhoda had tried to help Mum because she knew first aid and Granny M had called Rhoda a hero and somehow it felt true but it also felt wrong because Mum was still dead.

I take scissors to my suit that evening. I cut the

jacket to inky shreds like the feathers of a crow and I think people might shout but Granny M just holds me tightly and Dad doesn't say a word because he doesn't know what to say and neither do I.

12 15 19 20

It's been ten days since Mum died. Max goes back to
school straight after half-term quick as a flash because
he needs his routine but I don't so I stay in bed. I
want to hide in my attic space but I can't go up those
stairs and into that room that used to be hers so I stay
in my room and use my red notebook but instead of
working on my family tree I write down words in
code. Granny M gets Max ready in the morning and
he trots to his bus to see Rhoda and I wonder how
much he even knows.

But when he gets home in the afternoon he
scampers around looking for Mum and the
next morning he charges into Mum
and Dad's bedroom and he

searches for her. I know now it wasn't his fault that Mum was so grey and tired and poorly and I want to make it up to him, to whisper I'm sorry over and over and over and over again into the curve of his ear but I don't know how to start the words.

The next day when Angelique comes Max won't look at the picture cards. He turns his head away and when she offers him the spinning blue windmill without even asking for the card in exchange he won't take it. He clambers into her lap and he sits there still like a statue with his fingers tangled together and his eyes are staring at something that isn't there while Angelique strokes his hair.

1 12 15 14 5

It's been seventeen days since Mum died. The air
around me is empty. Mark rings the bell at the same
time every afternoon to ask if I'd like to walk Neil and
at the same time every afternoon I don't go. I
haven't left the house since the funeral.
Jamie and Ahmed knock after
they've finished school
and I don't want to
see them because they're
exactly the same and nothing
else is. I sit in my room and I hold
that glass orb paperweight we bought at
the flea market and I gaze at the galaxies on my
walls and I try not to break into a thousand pieces.

19 9 12 5 14 20

It's been twenty-three days since Mum died and time is still broken and loopy and jumpy and wild. I haven't been back to school. Mrs Havering sent one of the sympathy cards and now she sends work to me but I don't do it and Dad doesn't make me. He hasn't been back to work. He smells sour and he sits on the sofa in his dressing gown all day. The house is still and quiet and it feels frozen. I don't speak and Dad doesn't speak and the visitors start to drain away until it's just the three of us. Granny M starts to talk about me going back to school and I hear her say *Fred he needs to get back in his routine, he needs things to go back to normal* and Dad doesn't say anything but he's thinking the same as me that nothing will ever be normal again.

But the next day Granny M comes into my room and she throws back the curtains and lets the morning light drown my eyes. She lays out my fresh clean uniform on the bed and tells me in a sing-song voice that breakfast is waiting for me and I need to get up so I won't be late for school. I don't want to go and I can't go because I'll cry in front of everyone and if I leave this house then I'll come back and it'll still be empty and wrong. But Granny M cheerfully pulls my duvet off and I move my limbs through treacle so that I'm standing upright. *Good boy* she says softly and strokes my cheek just like Mum used to do.

And so I go back to school and I don't say a word. Everyone comes to see me and their eyes are wide and Sam gives me his favourite Match Attax card and a girl I don't even know hugs me so tight that the air pops in my lungs.

At break, all the footballers get into huddles to talk

tactics before kick-off and I follow like a robot. I am jostled and squeezed by the arms and elbows and shoulders holding me upright. I can barely breathe and I want to break out and sprint away across the playground and scale the metal fence and keep going until my muscles burn and my heart stops but I can't make my legs work.

Then the huddle breaks up and I haven't heard a word and I won't know the tactics. The footballers scatter to their positions but Noah stays right there beside me and he leans into my ear and he whispers *sorry to hear about your Mum, Frank. Still, at least your brother won't even notice the difference, will he?* He says it so low that the words are almost carried away on the wind before they reach me but they do and they swirl through my ears and into my brain. And as Noah walks away and shouts *on my head* and the ball bounces over to him like a crashing meteor whirling through the blank space I'm spinning off into, all I can see is Max leaping through the house looking for her and howling his brokenboy howl because she's not there and I don't

204

score a single goal and I don't say a single word.

I don't speak when Jamie comes round to play. I don't speak when Mrs Havering asks me the answer to a maths question and then she thinks I don't know. I don't speak when Max pushes his thumbs into my eyes and the world explodes inside my lids. I don't speak when Granny M asks me if I'd like to go and choose a present for Angelique's birthday. I don't speak when Max melts all over the kitchen floor because the mugs on the shelf don't look the same as usual except they do to everyone else so we don't know how to fix it and he screams and screams and screams. I don't speak I don't speak I don't speak I don't speak I don't speak I don't speak except in my head where the words for what I am feeling scribble themselves again and again and again but I can't say them out loud.

I use codes instead of using my voice but no one can crack them.

dot-dot-dot d a s h-d a s h-d a s h dot-dot-dot

Mum would know, but she's not here to tap back.

I'm not clever enough to make a code that sews the whole universe together but even the golden ratio doesn't give me a fizzing buzz any more because Mum dying doesn't fit, it's not part of a perfect pattern. It doesn't make sense. I don't write codes because I can't make the words say what I want them to. I am scared of my silence because something is stuck in me like the candyfloss in my teeth and I can't unstick it any more and I can't make the words come out. Max doesn't like it because it's different and he puts his hands on my face and he squashes me and tries to squeeze my voice out.

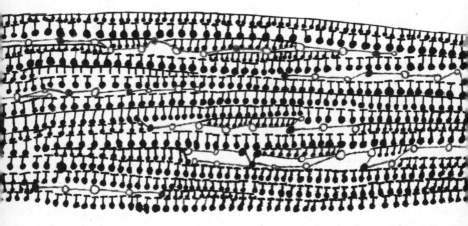

19 15 18 18 15 23

It's been twenty-eight days since
Mum died. Granny M and Dad are
having an argument in the kitchen and their
voices are bouncing up through the ceiling into
my room. I can hear snatches of fury and sorrow and
I can hear Granny M's voice rising through the floorboards and seeping through the cracks and she says
she wouldn't want this for her boys, you have to stop,
you have to start looking after them and I can hear his
sob-softened voice snaking up the stairs and he says *I*
can't do this without her, I can't do any of this without
her, you just don't understand.

I put my fingers in my ears just like Max
does when he hears things he can't

stand and I don't hear Max slip into my room and I don't realise until he puts his skinny arms around my neck and buries his dirty face into my shoulder. He twirls his fingers in my hair and the crescent nails are black with dirt and he makes a low whimpering sound. I put my arms tight around him and I want to make it all OK and I say *it's OK* with my hands and I say *it's OK* with my broken, unused voice that unsticks itself in that moment. And even as I say it, I can hear Dad's voice rising again in furious waves against the floorboards.

Granny M goes to stay with her sister.

6 1 18

1 16 1 18 20

That weekend Dad doesn't know what to do with Max and Max doesn't know what to do with Dad. They move around each other like wolves, circling and nervous. Dad tries to get Max to wear clothes and to eat food and to take a bath and to sit still, but Max doesn't want to do any of those things so he doesn't and he's grey and grubby and sad. Max is fading away and I don't know how to help him and I'm not sure if I have the energy inside me to try. I want Mum to come walking into the kitchen, smelling of cinnamon and sugar and I want her to take Max by the hand and run him a colour-streaked bubble bath and scrub away his grime and tears and then I want her to wrap us both up in thick blankets and sit next to us on the sofa while she tells us a story from inside her own head and draws the pictures to go with it. I want to cuddle into her soft warmth and I want it so badly that I can feel the ache in my chest like a bruise.

Max and Dad and I have fallen apart and there's no one to pick up the pieces and glue us back together again. Max spins further and further away from me and Dad is far away across the galaxy and I can't reach out and touch them.

18 15 1 13 9 14 7

2 3 9 12 4

It's been thirty-four days since Mum died. The food
in foil trays stops arriving and the cards stop coming
through the door. The world spins on and we are
trapped in the same space and the same place. My
school uniform is always dirty and crumpled and I
can't work out how to use the washing machine
and when I try I shrink my jumper. Dad goes
back to work but he finishes early every day
because he hasn't got anyone to be there
when Max gets home from school but
Dad being there doesn't make a
difference because Max just
roams and Dad
just lets

him and even Angelique can't get him to sit down and look at picture cards or toys with glitter spinning inside them. Granny M comes round but the creaks in her bones mean she can't help Max when he melts with a fury we've never seen before. He scribbles on the doors and rips pillows until there's feather snow tumbling through the air.

13 **5** 12

20

4

15 2**3** 14

It's been forty days since Mum died. We go to the supermarket because the pasta bakes and the stews have all gone and there's nothing in the fridge when I open it except an old dried lemon that is as light as air when I pick it up. The freezer has frozen over with ice and I imagine I'm an intrepid mountaineer chipping away at a sheer cliff face as I try to open the drawers and see if there's anything at all for us to eat but there isn't and my hands go purple and Dad sees the ice storm on the floor. For a moment I think he'll shout but he just sits down and rubs his hands across his sandpaper beard and Max hates the noise. I think

Dad will stay slumped on the sofa for the rest of the evening and I'll eat cornflakes with no milk for supper and pretend it's dehydrated space food again.

But then he stands up and says *we need to go out and get some food*. There's no one to have Max while we go and I think this isn't going to work but when I say it Dad snaps at me and says that *he'll just have to cope*. I wait for him to show Max the *coat and shoes* card and the *shops* card and he doesn't and he starts to get the coats and shoes anyway and then I know it won't work.

I scrabble through the plastic squares and I find the right ones and I fumble and stick them on to a Velcro strip in Max's special book and try to show them to Max but he's not used to me doing it and he's not sure. I put *biscuit* on the end and I say *first coat and shoes then shops then biscuit* and he pulls *biscuit* off and gives it to me. He's getting too clever for this and I don't know what to do.

Come ON Frank shouts Dad and he doesn't say it loudly in the way he would if he thought

I might not hear him. He shouts it like I'm doing something wrong and Max screams and I swallow until my throat is dry and clicking.

Dad wrestles Max into the car and he wrestles him out of the car and Max screams all the way there and he screams all the way through Sainsbury's. The lights are too bright and there's no list and Dad tries to put things in the trolley and hold on to Max while he melts down and down and down. Everyone looks at the wild-eyed bearded man in dirty clothes and the wild-eyed little boy with a dirty face and a too-small stripy T-shirt with Quaver dust sprinkling its seams and I try to disappear but they're looking at me too. Dad is trying to sing to Max in a raspy tuneless voice and he's trying to tell him what's happening and that we needed things like crisps and beige food and things for my lunchbox but Max is far, far away and the words echo round the aisles and fade away.

11 19
18
1
16
19

It's been forty-three days since Mum died. Weekends are long and slow and painful and I keep myself curled up in my room reading my *Beano* comics from the flea market or playing *Minecraft* on the cracked iPad when it's not keeping Max quiet. But today I go to Ahmed's house for the first time since everything became empty even though Ahmed's mum was one of the people who brought food round every day and she always had a different comic for me and a little spin-ning toy for Max and I don't think I ever even said thank you.

Ahmed's house is different to Jamie's because Jamie only has one brother and their house is quite like

Mark's with white walls and grey furniture and everything in a precise place. Mum said Jamie's house was beautiful and how clever his parents were to keep it so neat and clean with two children barrelling about. We went there for Christmas drinks once and Mum kept Max in a grip like a vice because there were so many beautiful things for him to shake and drop and rip. Max kept reaching out for a teardrop of glass filled with the flecks of a rainbow and so when he turned his head to look at the other treasures I moved it to a shelf and behind a picture of Jamie's mum and dad on their wedding day.

Jamie's mum kept laughing and saying *let him go, it doesn't matter* and so Mum released him while she had a cup of hot red spiced wine from a mug that was made of copper and didn't even have a handle. Max immediately pressed his fingers into the soft circle of a Very Expensive speaker and made a little mouse hole. Mum went the same colour as the wine in her handleless mug and Jamie's mum said it was fine but it wasn't really because Max had broken something important and we didn't take him back again.

There are no expensive speakers or delicate drops of glass in Ahmed's house. It is very loud and full of people and squashy sofas and the walls are covered in bright pictures and draped with swirls of material. Someone is always shouting and someone is always laughing and someone is always cooking and everyone always wants to give Ahmed a hug or pinch his cheek even though he's ten. There's always so much going on that you can just blend into the noise and the movement and the whirling of people all around you and as soon as I step through the door I sink back into my old self just a little bit and leave the motherless boy at home in the quiet cold air of our lifeless house.

Ahmed and I try to play videogames but his little cousins and nephews and nieces are there and they keep giggling and running across the room in front of the screen because they're playing some mad game involving imaginary crocodiles. And instead of getting cross and shouting at them like I would if Max was ruining my games, Ahmed throws himself on the ground and roars like he thinks a crocodile might roar and then he swims across the carpet. He snaps at their heels and thrashes his legs like a tail and the children jump up and down in a fizzing mix of fear and delight and a laugh escapes me and surprises us all.

I come home from Ahmed's with the laugh still fizzing a bit inside me like a tiny spark. I push open the door to my room and it's all wrong. I didn't remember to clicklock the padlock on my room with 2302 and no one remembered to do it for me. My football duvet is ripped and my *Beano*s are torn into tiny little rainbow snowflakes on my floor. My trophies are snapped and cracked and there are swipes of pen on my walls and my books are scattered in paper puddles. My books are my best thing because I breathe in the words that Mum used to read to me and they swirl in my head and I can click them together and pull them apart and make them sound just how she did and I can't breathe when I see what he's done. Everything is ruined.

A sparkle of light catches my eye and sprinkled on

the carpet like shards of a rainbow is the glass from the paperweight orb that Mum bought me at the flea market. It was just right, it was perfect, it fitted in and now it's broken and ruined and fractured and I let my feelings fly out of my mouth and I roar.

The roar is like something I've never heard from inside me and Dad runs in and stops dead but I slip past him quicksmart and I know where I'm going.

I thud down the stairs and reach into Max's special box where we keep all his treasures like his spinners and glittery balls and I pull out his stupid *Baby's Catalogue* that he loves so much with its folded pages and crinkled spine. I tear at it but it's too hard so I stand on it and rip it that way and I use my teeth like a wildboy and I don't stop even when Dad comes in and wraps his arms around me and lifts me up and away with my legs kicking and I hold on to the catalogue and when he tries to pull it from me it softly splits all along the middle and I don't stop until it's nothing and broken and ruined just like my room and

220

now maybe Max'll understand.

And then I am shouting and Max is hopping through the house and his fingers twitch and shuffle and click for his catalogue because he needs to thumb its pages and flick the corners and push his nose into the pictures so the inky smell flies into his brain and makes him smile. He hops and hops and hops and each lollop is faster and more desperate until the rubber band inside him pings and snaps and Max is melting into fury and sobs and it's all my fault and I feel rockets launching in my tummy.

Dad pulls him tight in our bear hug. Dad tells him he's going to get him a new *Baby's Catalogue* as soon as the shops open tomorrow but Max isn't listening and he doesn't know when the shops open and he wants the catalogue that I shredded into a million angry pieces. And I want to scream and scream but Dad keeps his arms around us and holds us so close that I can feel his heart and my heart and Max's heart beating together in a drumming symphony. I try to struggle free but he keeps me close and I draw in huge juddery lungfuls of air until my muscles start to thaw and I feel myself relaxing into the warmth of his body and he keeps on holding me and we cry together and Dad says *oh my boys my boys* while Max runs his fingers along our tears.

That night Dad puts Max to bed with a story and the right way of tucking his duvet all around his little body. Then we tidy up my room together and Dad sweeps away the razor-sharp rainbow shards of glass. When everything is in plastic bags and I've got a different cover on my bed, Dad tucks me in too and even though I'm ten, he reads me a story anyway.

The next day my uniform is washed and ironed and waiting for Monday.

6   18   19
      15   5   19 20

It's been fifty-two days since Mum died and it's
Christmas time everywhere but our house. Our
classroom windows are iced with sprayed-on snow
    and there's a fat tree with spikey splayed
        branches in the assembly hall. Year Six
            are allowed to decorate it and Mrs
                Havering gets us all to help
                cart huge brown boxes
                overflowing with bright
            tinsel and glittering baubles. I
        have been trying to ignore the lurching
    and whirling that gnaws in my tummy whenever
I think about Christmas and New Year and all those
empty years stretching ahead of me that put more

and more space between me and Mum. I hang baubles and I drape tinsel and I string fairy lights and while I'm doing it I try my absolute very best to switch my brain off but it won't listen and it gets louder and louder until I go into the loo and switch on the hand dryer just to try to drown out the roar.

It's the last day of term and when the bell rings out its goodbye I don't want to go home because the last day of the Christmas term is the day Mum and I would go together and choose a Christmas tree. She would always want to take a straggly bedraggled one with brown needles and droopy branches that were already sweeping the floor. She said she felt sorry for those trees and they looked like they needed a loving home but I always wanted the fresh bright green trees that smelt like the Wilderness.

When I stomp into the house Dad is sitting at his computer and Max is holding a clear plastic snowman filled with little puffs of snowglitter. It's new and Dad says Rhoda gave it to him for Christmas and Max holds it out so I can look at the snowstorm trapped inside the plastic. I can feel the disappointment burning in my bones but I don't say anything and I put the TV on too loud and Max clamps his hands over his ears and wails and his snowman rolls away from him. I click the volume up even higher to cover the sounds of his screams and I wish I could run up to the attic but I can't go up there now because it was hers.

Dad looks up from his computer and he says *Frank what are you doing you're upsetting him*. And I think what about me

what about me

what about me

and then the words fall out of my brain and into my mouth and I'm shouting.

Dad closes his laptop and he says *what's this all about* and I let the words bubble out and I tell him about the tree.

Dad goes round to Mark's and when he comes back there are two sets of footsteps. Mark is in our hall and Dad says *come on then, we've got ourselves a Max-sitter*.

Dad drives me to the place where Mum and I used to buy our tree and it's just us in the car and I can't remember that before. I put music on the radio and we sing along and we both sound terrible and that makes us laugh and sing louder and it sounds even worse.

There aren't that many trees left because we're so close to Christmas but there are still some that fill the air with the wildness of the woods. I wander round and try to choose one but not one of them feels right. Dad says *come on Frank, which one do you think?* And I keep walking through the forest until I get right to the very back where all the lonely brown trees are hiding and I say *these ones, these ones please*.

The man doesn't even want to sell us one brown Christmas tree and he says they're only good for the chipper and my heart lurches at the thought of them being chopped to smithereens and I say *please please please*. And he rolls his eyes and says we can just have them if we want and I look at Dad and he rolls his eyes too and it takes us forever to cram six trees into

226

the car and when they're in there they look like all the colours of a bonfire.

At home I make a forest in our living room. Max isn't sure at all at first because this is all new and it's not how it's supposed to look but I put batteries into the colour-changing lights and flick the switch and it's like a magic spell. I get out the glittery baubles and Max reaches out his hands to feel. I show him how to loop the lights round and round the branches so that the trees twinkle and throw rainbow shapes on to the walls.

On Christmas Day we sit in our forest and we miss her.

Then the fireworks boom and blast us into a whole new year and I feel like we're leaving her behind.

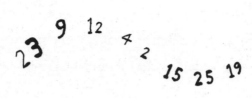

It's been sixty-seven days since Mum died
and on the last day before we go back to
school after the holidays it snows. Thick and
white and pillowy and it ices the houses and
hangs heavy from tree branches. I want to
take my sledge with its horn and its lights to
the Wilderness. But it's only daylight for a
flash and then dark lickety-split quick so
going to the Wilderness lasts only as long as
it takes for the sun to drop and buttery melt
into the sky. I go down the cold dark steps to
the cellar and I drag it up from the damp
spider-scuttling depths all by myself and
then I call Jamie and Ahmed to come over.

Max sees me putting on my big coat and my thick hat and bright yellow gloves and he doesn't like it at all. Jamie and Ahmed look at the screamy Max stretching his hands out for me and Ahmed says *mate, let your brother come with us*. And I don't feel that white-hot swish of anger and disappointment like I did when Mark said that all those months ago and I say *OK* and I get Max's cards to show him and I don't hide them from Ahmed and Jamie.

I pull Max to the Wilderness on my sledge and he presses his hands together in joy and his face is split with a smile. Dad and Max have to come as a pair but Dad says he's not really there but he definitely is. He sits on a frozen tree stump and takes out a book to pretend to read while he watches Max in case he melts before the sun does.

Max is a jumping bean and he runs and whoops and tumbles down the twisty snowy wilderness paths and I burn with worry and shame but Ahmed runs and whoops too and then Jamie and then I try it and I shout out all of the noises in my head and this is the wildest we've ever been and we are four wildboys in a wild wood. We make a racket and a din and a riot and Max doesn't push his fingers in his ears or bite his hands or smash his head on the frosty floor.

I put him in front of me on the sledge and Ahmed gives us a shove and suddenly we are shooting down the snowy hillside, the sleek silver skis of my sledge cutting perfect lines in the crunchy white beneath us. Max is whooping and he puts his hands over mine as I steer the sledge to the bottom and we tumble off in a soft heap. We run back to the top and my mouth is stretched wide and I'm having fun with Max. I can see Dad sitting watching us on his tree stump and I can't be sure because he's a miniature man in the distance but I think I see him smiling.

Our breath makes cold milky clouds in
the air and we puff our cheeks and
blow smoky streams because
it makes Max laugh
and he huffs
out

231

his own air and catches it in his hands. Then Max holds out his hands for Ahmed and Jamie and I burn again because only babies hold hands but then they just take them and it's suddenly so simple. Max has no hands left so I hold Jamie's hand and we run down the hill in a string of arms and a tangle of legs and a burst of brilliant impossible happiness just for that sliver of a second.

When we get home Dad makes us all hot chocolate, even Max, and Max copies Jamie when he blows across the top of it to cool it down. He sticks his tongue into the brown milk and a look of pure shock flashes on his face but he doesn't melt. I don't say anything to Jamie and Ahmed about Max not ever drinking hot chocolate and Dad smiles at him and tells him he's a good boy and he does it with his voice and his hands. Dad sits with us at the table and he teaches us how to play a card game called blackjack. We use buttons to bet with while Max tongue-pokes his cooling drink. I get to use maths and a bit of luck and I win the biggest pile of rainbow-coloured buttons.

Darkness is spilling through the kitchen window before it feels like something's missing again and my heart is squeezed hollow.

19 20
15
18
9
5
19

It's been sixty-nine days since Mum
died and we're back to school after the
strange and wild and brilliant and awful
bursts of time that spun around me over
Christmas. We're still working on our Big Project.
I sit in the first lesson we have on it since I came
back to school and I burn inside and I want to scream
and scream that my family is ragged and torn apart. I
think about the little cross next to a name that means
someone has died and I think if I have to make those
two simple lines next to Mum's name then I will
die as well. I stare into space for the whole
lesson and I don't let the nib of my pen
touch the paper of my notebook.

✝

234

People keep looking at me sitting there, doing nothing, but I just keep blinking away the tears and Mrs Havering doesn't come over and tell me to get on with my work.

When I'm changing in the cloakroom for PE I hear Lucy and Meggie whispering in the corridor that Mrs Havering didn't make me do any work because my mother died and it would be *insensitive* to make me keep writing about families when I don't have a proper one any more. I swallow the hot lump of rage that rises in my throat and pull my polo over my head. I think about the little books I made last term with my illustration that Jamie said was the best he'd seen and the lesson I spent carefully writing out the tiny details that built up the picture of my family that has now been shattered into a million pieces. I think about the Family Forest that we're going to make and the cardboard and papier mâché trees that will line the walls of the hall with the stories of all the normal families hanging from their branches.

I pull on my plimsolls and then I creep back into

the now-empty classroom. The playing field is filling up with my class, a scatter of PE tops and the thump of footballs. I reach into my tray and I pull out the stories I've finished. I don't look at the picture of Mum and Dad and instead I shove them all deep into the bottom of the bin underneath the pencil shavings and breaktime banana skins.

The next day Mrs Havering makes me stay behind when the bell rings for breaktime. I don't look at her and instead I stare straight over her shoulder out of the window and I know I'm being rude but I know she's going to ask how I'm doing and if she can do anything and I know I might shout if she does that. But she doesn't. Instead she opens her desk drawer and nestled among red pens and rulers and half-open notebooks with important-looking writing scribbled between their lines are my family storybooks. I don't ask her how she found the books all buried under the rubbish of a day. I look at Mrs Havering and she's not saying anything and for a heart-lurching moment I think I'm in deep trouble for throwing away my work

236

and I can feel hot tears threatening to spill.

But Mrs Havering doesn't shout. She doesn't tell me that throwing away my work was a wicked thing to do and she doesn't tell me that I've got to litter-pick from now until the end of term. She tells me about her daughter.

Mrs Havering only put her son, Laurie, on the family tree that she sketched on the whiteboard all those months ago before the sky fell in. She didn't fill in the branch next to him because her daughter died before she was even born. *Stillborn*, Mrs Havering says and her voice jumps a little. Her name was Isabel and she was Laurie's little sister. Mrs Havering says she would be thirty-two now and that every year on her birthday she puts a spray of snowdrops on her grave and remembers her little life that never got to begin. And I remember Mrs Havering telling us that *every life had a story that's longer and more complex than we ever imagine, even a tiny baby*. And I know she was talking about Isabel.

Mrs Havering says that she was wrong not to put

237

Isabel on the tree because her life was important and it mattered and she would never forget her and neither would Laurie or her husband or even Laurie's wife and their children. They will all grow up with her and without her. And then she tells me that even though my heart must be breaking into a thousand million pieces that I should tell the story of my mother and the story of my family.

21 14 9 22 5 18 19 5
19 11 25 19 16 13 5 3
15 19 13 15 19 7 1 12
1 24 25 19 20 1 18 19

The next weekend I get up early. Mum's
studio smells musty and old and very faintly
of something that makes my heart lurch. No one
has been up here since she died. It's different now
but it's just like I remembered, all at once. Tubes of
paint and big tables and jars and brushes and some
blank canvases with faint pencil lines scarring their
skin. There are paintings that I don't think I've
ever seen before leaning against the wall. I move
them apart more carefully than I've ever moved
anything ever and I see something half-finished but
completely us.

It's Mum and Dad is standing behind her
with his hands resting on her sloping

239

shoulders. There's a little boy sitting on her lap, wearing a stripy T-shirt and holding something tight in his fist. And there's a bigger boy with curly hair standing next to her holding her hand and she's smiling like a whisper in the quietest, sweetest curve of lips and she shines from the canvas. There are patches where she hasn't painted in the colour and the canvas is shock white where some of our skin should be but it doesn't matter one bit.

I breathe it all in and I feel like I can almost touch her. I look at the gentle curve of Mum's lips and the delicate tiredness that she's blushed under Dad's eyes and Max's skinny knees and my cheek pressed tight against her side holding my old red motorbike in my other bony hand. Whatever Max is holding in his fist is just a sketchy outline and my T-shirt is just a white gap and Dad's hands are skeletal grey lines. I puzzle at the shape in Max's hand until I see the ridges and swirls of the ammonite I bought him from the Science Museum when I was in Year Five.

I stare at the blank unpainted space until my

eyes blur but I can see it now. Pencilled numbers strung together into codes, some peeping and spiralling out from behind paint, some stark and alone on the white canvas. Codes that unlock the swirl of feelings and memories I keep trapped in my chest and make them into something more magical. This is the canvas where I used to scribble my secret thoughts before she died and I couldn't come up here any more.

I haven't been up here since weeks before she died. She must have been making this painting for us when she said she was clearing things out. When she said she wanted to start painting again, she started with us. I can feel tears rippling at the edges of my eyes because she never got to finish it and now we'll never be complete. I pick up a pencil and with a trembling hand and in the lightest strokes possible I write all the codes I've been scribbling in the back of the red family tree notebook instead.

I carry the painting downstairs just as the sun starts to push gently through morning mist. I am so careful and I barely breathe as I hold it aloft and angle it so it doesn't bash into the banisters or the wall. I lean it against the hall table. Then I make some coffee using the special plunging pot that Dad always used to use on lazy Sunday mornings and fill the house with something that smelt so delicious that I begged to try it and it was disgusting and I was so disappointed and confused. It smelt rich and deep and so grown-up and it tasted bitter and like your mouth when you've just been sick. Mum thought that that was really funny but not as funny as the look on my face when I tried it and she asked me to try it again so she could take a picture. I look at the framed photo of me that is sitting on the mantelpiece and my eyes are crossed and my tongue is stuck out and you can almost hear me saying *yuck*.

I pour the hot water on to the coffee really carefully and then I take the whole thing next door. I have to leave everything on the doorstep while I go and get the painting. It nearly blocks the whole of the doorway and I ring the bell.

1 18 20

Mark opens the door and he's wearing pyjamas and a dressing gown and his face is crumpled on one side and I think it must be very early. I think about turning around and scuttling back into my house but he smiles when he sees me and says *thank goodness you thought to bring coffee.*

Mark brings in the painting and rests it carefully against his sofa. He goes and puts on jeans and a jumper and then he sits at the kitchen table and pours the coffee into two of his white mugs. I blink away the blue-siren-stained images from that terrible afternoon and I sniff my coffee but I don't drink it. Mark says I'm probably a bit young to drink coffee let alone enjoy it and he'd trained himself to like it over many years. Then he fetches a jug and stirs in milk and two fat lumps of brown sugar into my cup and it tastes a lot better after that.

And even though Mark must know, I tell him about Mum and how she could paint the most terrible things, the most boring things, the most ugly things and she could turn them into something beautiful. I tell him about the smell of paint on her shirt and how the colours made the air taste. I tell him about the top bedroom and the arrival of Max and the closed door and the dusty stairs and the way the paint faded from the air. I tell him about the screaming in Sainsbury's and what Noah said and Mrs Havering's Isabel and the family stories. And I tell him my plan.

Mark stirs his coffee even though he hasn't put any milk or sugar in it. He takes a sip and he doesn't pull a face like I would. And he says *OK*.

I don't want to start small but Mark says we have to otherwise it'll all go wrong because I won't know how to use the paint properly. *It's not like poster paint* he says and I need to know *what to do.* So he shows me. He takes me upstairs to his top room where the light is perfect and he shows me his studio. It is very different to the rest of his house. Up here there's no white or grey or twisty bits of metal sculptures that look too delicate to breathe near. There's a shiny computer on a tiny desk and Mark says that's where he does his designing work, but that's not what I'm looking at. There are hundreds of jars half-filled with water and tubes of paints squiggling across great big tables and brushes of every size sprouting from tins like flowers. There are big canvases with sweeping brushstrokes rippling across them and tiny canvases where the brush has just nibbled across the surface.

I pull out a scrap of paper from my pocket and lay it on a work table. *I want to do this* I say. And

Mark just nods again.

Mark shows me how to mix paints and tries to get me to copy so that I can get the colours I like. It's harder than it looks. I think that my plan might not be the best idea in the world. The names of the paints sound so strange and yet like I've always known them and I roll them around on my tongue. *Cad-mee-umm. Oh-cah. Ali-zar-in. Ul-tra mah-reen.*

Mark says it's not a problem if the colours don't match his as long as I like them. He makes me write down how much I used of each colour when I find a mixture I like and soon I have pages of torn paper covered with soft grey pencil scribbles.

Mark gives me a tiny canvas the size of a postcard. He shows me how to sketch out my drawing first so that I know where I have to paint and which lines to fill. This is just a practice so I sketch out Neil and then we find greys and blacks and whites to mix into the shades of his fur. Mark helps me with the brushstrokes and Neil's paintfur starts to look like his real fur and I can almost feel its wiry coarseness rising up from the canvas.

The next bit is more difficult.

We have to go and get Max.

Max is up and eating Quavers in his spacepants and so I get him dressed as quickly as you can ever get Max dressed. Dad just sits on the sofa staring at the blank TV screen and he doesn't seem to notice us scampering around him or me chasing Max with a pair of trousers.

Max loves Mark and he loves Neil but I don't have a picture card for next door and if I show him the card for Neil he'll think we're going for a walk. I load up the computer and click through until I find the right picture card for *next door* which is just two doors with an arrow pointing to one of them and I don't think it's going to be very helpful. The printer whirrs and spits out the message for Max and I show it to him. He puts his head on one side like a curious baby bird and I take his hand and try to lead him out of the door but he starts to stiffen and his arms are flapping like a crow. His mouth opens and he shrieks and he drops to the floor into a puddle.

I go back next door and I tell Mark it won't work *at all*. He puts his head on one side just like Max and he's thinking and then he says *if Max won't come to the mountain then the mountain will come to Max* and I haven't got a clue what he's talking about but then he grabs some huge bags and starts loading painting things into them and I think I get it.

I return home and explain to Max what we are doing. He looks right at me and his dark eyes are like liquid pools that deepen as I speak. I want to hold him close to me then but I know he'd yelp so I just keep talking and he nods and his little hands flap but in the gentle way that means he's excited. And we bound up the stairs to Mum's studio.

We sketch together. Mark helps us mix paints and choose brushes and cleans them when they get clumped with colour. Max and I draw the outlines of planets and the cosmos and swirling showers of comets and arcs of light that might be somewhere deep in space and pinprick dots of stars and Max is lying flat on Mum's big canvas Mark brought back over and his tongue is poking out in concentration and I've never seen him so still.

We fill in the gaps.

We fill them with colour and light and space and patterns and patchwork.

We paint nervously at first with little dabs and drips and then we make our marks stronger and bolder and the gaps close. I cover my codes with paint but I know they're there and they're nestled between then and now.

We fill our universe and our galaxy and our cosmos and our world with splashes and spots and streaks and strokes of paint. In the swirls of a galaxy I hide the dots and dashes that make up our secret Morse code message to each other. We make colours that are bright and deep and dark and dull and shining and we paint and paint until the whole of the canvas is teeming with the space we've made. It is one of the most beautiful things I have ever seen and Mark holds it up for us and we are lost in the depth of the universe.

It looks different.

It looks jumbled.

It looks just right.

Dad is still sitting on the sofa when we come downstairs and he's still watching a TV that isn't on. Mark tells him we have something to show him and Dad looks up like he's surprised that Mark is here even though Mark has made him three cups of tea today and said that he's looking after Max.

Max and I grab Dad's hands and they feel papery and dry but we pull him to his feet and we take him upstairs. When we get to the winding stairs that go all the way to the top of the house he stops and it's like there's a sheet of glass in front of him and he can't get through it. But Max shatters the glass with a yelp of excitement and we climb.

Mark has propped the painting up against the wall on top of one of the big tables. It's dark in the studio now and the painting is us and it's shining in the dim. *We did it* I say to Dad. *We did it together for Mum.*

We weren't just her world but we were her universe and her space and her stars and her sky and her galaxy and her cosmos too whispers Dad and he wraps his arms around us and draws us to him and he doesn't let go for a long time and I can feel him crying but I'm not scared. We have filled in the empty sketched spaces with all of the universe, together.

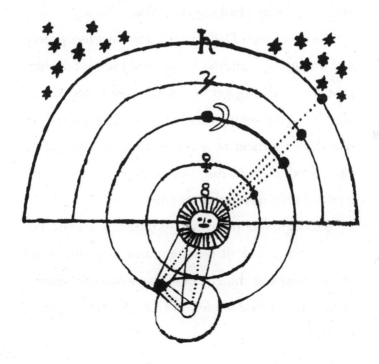

5   **1**2

5   **22**

5   *14*

It's one hundred and nineteen days since Mum died and this is harder even than Christmas because there are crocuses pushing their yellow heads through the soil in the garden and Mum planted the bulbs when I was born. They're my birthday flowers and when I clicked my bedroom padlock shut today 2302 was true because today I am eleven.

    Eleven should be the best age I've ever been because the numbers are the same whether you read them forwards or backwards and I've never had that before. But it doesn't feel right and there isn't the usual birthday
fizzing spark of joy
leaping in

my tummy because Mum isn't here and she always made my favourite cinnamon biscuits and my favourite chocolate cake and hung balloons from the ceiling where they couldn't rain down on Max and make him scream. We would have cake for breakfast and when I blew out the candles I'd close my eyes and make a wish and I burn when I think about the stupid things I used to want to come true. I'm in a whole new year and it's a whole new year that Mum doesn't exist in and it feels like she's falling behind.

When I go downstairs there's a funny rustling and I think Max must have got into the printer paper tray again and made snow. But when I go into the kitchen Dad is there and he's throwing streamers across the table and Granny M is there and she's wearing a pointy party hat and Max is grabbing handfuls of streamers and putting them where he thinks is best which is everywhere. And on the table along with the streamers is a chocolate cake and it's wonky and the buttons have started to slide off the icing but it's still my favourite.

They sing happy birthday quietly so Max doesn't shout and he signs *happy* at the end and we cheer for all the words he's slowly collecting. I ache for a cinnamon-sugar hug from Mum that creaks my bones but I swallow the feeling and Granny M gives me sweets to take to school.

At school Jamie gives me a new football and Ahmed gives me a wrapped box and he says I can't open it until I get home and that it's from him and his mum and dad and all his brothers and sisters too. I give it a little shake and I can hear a rattle inside but I don't know what it could be and I'm itching to tear off the birthday paper and find out.

At break I get to be football captain because it's my birthday and I score four goals with my new ball and I run round the pitch like a mad thing and everyone mobs me because I'm the boy with the magic foot-balling feet.

When I get home we have a birthday tea with lemonade in glass bottles with stripy straws and little cakes decorated with sugar-paste footballs and Max touches his tongue to one quick as a flash. Granny M gives me a book about spies and new football boots and Angelique has given me a torch for adventuring in the Wilderness. Her mum has sent me a tiny skateboard that you skate on with just your fingers and she's even sent Max a present. It's a funny plastic telescope which shows a thousand different colours that change their pattern when you shake it. He gazes inside it and watches the shapes falling and melting and twisting into something new and it is his best present ever.

Mark comes round and gives me two huge books all about space and I'm about to open Ahmed's present but Dad says *hold on* and then he disappears out of the room. When he comes back, he's holding a big box and he's wrapped it so badly that the birthday paper looks like it's been in a fight but it doesn't matter because I tear it off faster than a flash of light. It takes me a minute for my brain to work out what my eyes are seeing and when I do I whoop out loud and Max jumps but he doesn't melt.

It's a brand-new computer. For me.

Dad comes over and he's moving a bit like he's embarrassed and he says *I thought I could teach you coding, like we always said, would you like that?* And it's what I've wanted since I was tiny and it's what he's always said he'll teach me and I'm excited and squirmy with a kind of sadness that always seems to sit right in my chest and blooms like a bruise whenever anything happy happens.

And when I open the present from Ahmed's family there's an actual real-life robot nestled in a bright blue box and I know Dad must have been talking to Ahmed's mum because you can use computer codes to make this robot dance and spin and run and talk and I can't wait and excitement rises up and fizzes right to the ends of my fingers and the bruise fades, just a little.

2 3

9

12   4

The next day I have a
birthday party in the
Wilderness. Granny M ties
balloons to the trees and we
wrap the Christmas tree lights
into their branches and it looks
magical. We have a barbecue even
though it's February and there's frost
in the air and we eat wildboy burgers
and sausages and pretend they're rabbit.
Jamie and Ahmed come and bring their
families and there are children everywhere.
Angelique comes and Mark brings Neil who
sits by the barbecue and waits for sausages. We

257

run and we whoop and we sail through the air on our rope swing and I paint my face with streaks of mud and there is a flicker of Frank the wildboy again. In a quiet corner near an oak tree Ahmed and Jamie and I scratch our numbers into the dirt and make a pact to be friends forever and beyond.

Max stands with Dad with half an eye on the burning embers in the barbecue and half an eye on the running and jumping blurs of limbs that go flying past him while we play British Bulldog. He's wearing big earphones that Angelique brought round months ago and he's only just decided they're OK to have clamped over his ears instead of his hands and they block the noises that make him melt. He's still twisty and anxious and after an hour he starts to pull at his lips and gnaw on his hand and before he can become a puddle Angelique takes him home for tea.

We light a fire in a circle of stones and warm our hands by it as the stars start to blink and the day is dissolving. Granny M lights tiny candles inside lanterns and their glow makes our shadows loom and twist and we try to make shadow puppets but they all look like monsters with too many legs whenever we try to make animals. Dad brings out a huge birthday cake with twelve silver candles because there's one for luck and everyone sings happy birthday but there's a voice missing and no one tells me to make a wish and I'm glad.

I am eleven and I am a flicker of a wildboy once again and I am one year of age and one hundred and twenty days away from her.

The next day Mark and Neil and Max watch TV and Dad shows me a new language of numbers on the computer that can make my robot dance and it's more magical than the Wilderness in twilight.

23 9 12 4 20 8 9 14 7

It's been one hundred and twenty-two days since Mum died. We have a letter from Max's school. It isn't just a letter but an invitation to his school play and it has words in it like *educational* and *enriching* and *self-expression* and I ask Dad what that means. He says that *it's the way we act when we want to show others who we are and what we're feeling* but that doesn't make sense because Max always lets us know when he's happy and sad and angry. When Max is happy then he *is* happy and he's nothing else besides.

Every bit of his body flickers with sparks of joy and he's everything that it means to be happy in that moment. When Max melts each grain of his body feels his rigid hot anger like they're on fire and there's no space for anything else. I don't know how pretending to be somebody else in a play will help Max be himself.

Anyway I'm not sure why Max's school is doing a play at all because plays have lines to learn and words to say and new clothes to wear and all the things Max cannot do although he does put on his starry school top now. Dad says a play can *be whatever it wants to be* and I don't understand what he means but I will go anyway because I want to see the space-ship school.

Max has brought home the book that will be his play and it's his new most favourite book of them all and I'm glad because I ripped up his *Baby's Catalogue* and the new one we bought wasn't the same. The other children in his class will be Wild Things and he will be Max. He traces the pictures in the air and then he traces his name too and a M A X is penned with fingers.

And six days later at Ahmed's birthday in the

spring-dusted shivery cold garden with the liquid inky dark all around him he burns a wobbly letter M into the night with a sparkler and Dad cries. So does Ahmed's mum, and Jamie and Ahmed and I whoop into the echoey sky.

The Max in the book wears a wolf suit and sails far and away to the land of the Wild Things and they are terrifying and beautiful and monsters and kind and Book Max is a bit like them and a bit like a boy. Book Max is in a new land and the story says he's far away across the world from his home and he wants to go back and be loved and I think that's Real Boy Max sometimes and the more I turn the pages back and forth back and forth the more Book Max and Real Boy Max scribble over each other's lines.

Granny M makes Real Boy Max a Book Max wolf suit that's real too and it has a furry tail and clawed paws and pointy ears and when he sees it he draws it in the air and he doesn't shout when she helps him put it on because he's read the outfit a thousand times

and run his finger around its lines. He looks like Neil-the-dog and he looks like Book Max and he looks like Real Boy Max and he scamper-trots around the kitchen with clattery paws. He won't take it off even at bedtime and he holds the tail in his hand while he sleeps in his forest room and his treacly sleep heat sticks his hair to his wolf-hooded forehead.

I howl like a wolf when I see him in the morning. Max likes the howl and he pulls my hand until I do it again and he stares at me in his wolf suit with his boy eyes and then he howls too because it's a very Max-ish noise but it's the first time he's done the same sound as me.

Max is still a wolf when Angelique comes round and he shows her his book even though he's shown her before but this time he's showing her because he's Book Max today. Angelique is very pleased by this and she lets us howl in the kitchen and she even joins in and I laugh until my stomach aches with its happy balloon. And Max asks Angelique to read us the story when he hands over a plastic strip stuck with two squares and one says **I want** and the other is a picture of a book.

2 5 19 20

15 6

1 12 12

It's one hundred and forty-three days since Mum died. Max's class is doing their play in the morning because they won't like staying after school because that's too different to usual. I think that means that I won't be able to go but Dad rings Wolverton and talks to Mrs Havering and says he's taking me on an *educational visit* but he doesn't say what. Dad says to me that Max will want me there and that's that and I'm surprised but secretly definitely pleased too.

We take Granny M and Mark and Angelique and Mark drives us in his car that has a roof that can fold down when you touch a button. I touch the button quite a lot and Dad tells me to stop it but Mark just laughs and says how he did exactly that when he first bought the car. Mark wanted to come and see Max in his first proper acting role and Max definitely wanted Mark to come because Mark is one of his best people.

The spaceship school is made of whiteness. The walls are scrubbed clean empty nothingy white white white. The idea of Max with his stars and flashing squashy balls and light-up shoes and colour-changing windmill and bouncing walk pops bright against the blank. In Wolverton the corridors are jumbled with scribbly Year One drawings and a patchwork of paintings paving a path to the classrooms. I feel like my eyes are squinting into sunlight until I find the darkened room. It is the same one from the pictures I saw long ago with spinning lights and liquid tubes of bubbles stretching to the ceiling and it is the plug-hole draining all the colour of the school towards it.

Rainbows bounce off the mirrored walls and I stare and stare and stare at the shadows of fat globs of oil flicking the ceiling from a lamp in the corner and the fizz of a twirling ball made from coloured glass. It's magical like the pier in Brighton and splashes of white leak through the door from outside and become something beautiful. Dad says *Frank hurry up* and I pull my eyes away from the streaks of sparks. *Hurry hurry hurry hop hop hop* says Dad just like Mum used to and we walk through the nothing corridors to the hall and to Max.

We all sit in a big white hall on rickety rackety plastic chairs that rock when I move and I think of the time I tumbled and my arm went crack. My arm is knitted and fixed now but Sam broke his arm again last week when he jumped off the climbing frame and the doctor said his bones weren't as strong as before so I try to stay statue still on my difficult chair.

We watch two plays and they're not the same as the plays at Wolverton. The first class we see isn't Max's class and the children are a tangle of dressed-up bears and trees and people. There are thirty children in my class at Wolverton and there are seven in this one and five adults who are also dressed up like part of the play. I try to imagine Mrs Havering doing that and it's a strange thought and I can't shape the picture right in my head.

The children tramp on stage and stomp through paper fields of grass and wear squeaky clean wellies to squish squash through painted cotton-wool mud puddles. They are bigger than Max but they still flip flap and bounce on the little stage and some of them hold a grown-up's hand. Some of the trees have pressed themselves flat into the white wall at the back of the stage with their branch arms low and their heads to the side and eyes screwed tight but peeping through just enough to watch the bear hunt.

The teacher reads the words so the play has no lines but a story anyway and another teacher plays a piano and some of the bears have electric machines with big round buttons and sounds recorded on them and sometimes they press them and it's the perfect time and sometimes it's not but it still works. The mud sucks *shuck shuck shuck* at the welly boots and the grass swishes and then as a big surprise there's real water and a little boy with red hair uses a spray bottle to make the river splash. Rain falls on the audience and they clap but whisper-soft quietly so the bears and trees don't scream.

Then it's Max and no one reads the words because Max can tell this story all by himself even if he doesn't make a sound. I see him and I forget about my rickety chair and the white walls and misery and Mum and I just see Max. Max in his furry wolf suit. Max with his cardboard cut-out boat with painty fingerprints walking down the side and his wobbly M A X signature sloping away from him where he's raced through the alphabet to find his own code. Max with his bouncing wolf lollop and clattery claws. Max with his beaming smile stretching out forever on the map of his face. Max with his clawpaw clasping his teacher's hand

270

and then letting go and running free. Max is the only wolf boy on the stage and he twirls around his world finding Wild Things and sailing through ocean storms and rumpus dancing under an invisible starry sky until he wants to be somewhere where somebody loves him best of all and he takes a swooping bow and jumps off the stage and throws his arms around us.

After Max has clambered back on to the stage and sailed home in his private boat and the Wild Things have roared and clawed and gnashed and one has lain down on the floor and maybe one has gone to sleep we all clap and the plays are over.

The head teacher stands on the stage but she doesn't talk for ever and ever like Mrs Owens at Wolverton. She is wearing blue jeans and a bright green top with tiny white splodges and when I squint I can see that the splodges are cats. She says her name is Kate and she's pleased we could all come and see such *magnificent performances*. I'm surprised she is wearing jeans because teachers at Wolverton aren't allowed to do that and I'm even more surprised she said her first name because everyone knows that teachers guard their first names with their lives. Then Kate says she particularly enjoyed Max's performance especially his *improvisation* and the audience does a little laugh and we all shuffle upright in our wonky chairs and are puffed out with proudness.

Kate tells us we can go to the classrooms and have squash and biscuits with the actors and when she says *actors* I think it sounds funny but then I think it's true. So it's back into the blankwhite corridors blending into a blurry tunnel. There are no edges to the walls and ceiling.

Max's classroom is white too but the children in it are fireworks of colour and movement and noise. They jump and leap and twirl and flap and bounce and play with their voices so they squeak and growl and shriek and sing. One of them is making squash with a teacher and a boy smaller than Max is carefully balancing a plastic plate of biscuits in his hands and his tongue is stuck out with effort and concentration so he keeps forgetting to offer them to the visitors, who are us. I finally get a Jammie Dodger and I say thank you and then I remember and say thank you with my hands too and the little boy leaps up and down with jumping joy and I catch the falling biscuits.

Max's teacher is called Georgia and he loves her. He flings his skinny arms around her before he sees we are there and he looks up at her with big eyes like Neil when you have a piece of cheese. Georgia says to him that *Angelique and Granny and Daddy and Frank are here* and then she sees Mark and he holds out his hand and says he's our friend and he is. Max does a lollopy spin and sees me eating a Jammie Dodger and Mark and Angelique admiring a display board of finger-painted fireworks and Granny M and Dad holding plastic tumblers of orange squash.

Max's face is crumply and he's twisty and fizzy because it's not the play any more and he's in his classroom and this is wrong because we are home and this is school. Max's little hands start to flap down low and he *beep beep beeps* his voice as a warning. Georgia puts her hands on his sloping shoulders and

273

grips them and then presses down hard and I think that she's being too strong and Max's skinny boy body will buckle and fall but he stands up tall as she squeezes and sings a quiet song. It's different, it's strange, it's certainly a change, but there's no need to be afraid so be brave so be brave so be brave. The words are softly low and I dip my head and catch them in my ears and I hum along with the tune because it's one everybody knows but I don't know how.

And Max is calm.

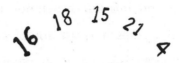

I have to go back to my school after Max's play
and Max's not-melting. The corridors and walls
are jumbly and messy and familiar and I trudge
back to learn about the Tudors for four minutes
before the lunch bell goes *brrrring ping ping*
and our flippy desks go slam and our feet stomp
and it sounds like music. Mrs Havering shouts
at us to walk not run but we don't really listen
and we scatter into the playground to wait for
Year Six's turn in the lunch hall. The footballers
start to divvy up teams and Sam shouts that
he'll be referee which is the official position of
anyone with a broken arm, which has only been
me and him so far, so he doesn't really need to

say it but Sam likes to shout.

We are in our tight knots of teams talking tactics because that's what the best players do. Noah is on our team because Jamie and Ahmed weren't pickers today and Kai was and Noah scores goals. Noah keeps saying *slide tackle slide tackle slam their legs* and I want him to shut up shut up shut up. I stop listening until Kai is bored with Noah shouting and asks me where I was all morning. I pause with a lie caught in my mouth and I swallow it back down and I can feel it sinking darkly and dissolving. I say *I watched my brother Max in his school play*. Noah pulls the face he thinks is like Max and he says *how can **that** even be in a play it can't even talk* and then he does his yelping laugh like the hyenas from cartoons.

Ahmed and Jamie clench their fists again but I just keep talking and talking and all the words and thoughts in my head spill out of my mouth and I listen to them for the first time. I say *he played Max and he went to the land of the Wild Things in his private boat with his very own name painted on it by*

Max and not a teacher and then I tell them about Max leaping off the stage because he loves us best of all and Max writing his name in fire in the starry night and his first word and that he can speak in a thousand ways without words and he can show all the moments of his day in just his face and his body talks in a way mine never can and he can be in a play and speak no words from his mouth and tell the whole story anyway and about him sledging down the wilderness hillside with us and his impossible infectious happiness and his rushing anger when the world is not his own and the colours and the noises and the changes that hurt like a million arrows and about the magic squeezing that calmed Max's raging fizzy body bees and head wasps and that Max is made of stardust and that I am proud.

He is Max and I am proud. I say it again. And again. And again.

And then I walk away.

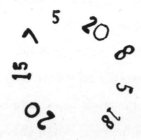

It has been one hundred and fifty-
four days since Mum died. It's the last
day of the first whole term I've had without
her. Tomorrow Ahmed and Jamie and I are going
to the Wilderness and I've made a promise to teach
them Morse code using my new torch to make long
and short flashes for dashes and dots so we can share
secret codes in the dark.

The Family Forest is dense with trees of all shapes
and sizes. Some of them are flat paper stuck on to the
walls and some of them are made from papier mâché
and they're 3D and stand up by themselves. Some
of them are made from cereal boxes and old
mops and have leaves made from

torn-up shopping bags and tinfoil and tissue paper whispering in a quiet breeze.

There are families milling around, walking through the wood and exclaiming when they see their own name or their photograph stuck on a book that hangs from a cardboard branch. Noah is keeping his head low and trudging behind his parents and I'm surprised to see him walking like that but his father strides ahead with a stony face like he doesn't want to be here at all. Jamie's mum is giving him a hug and all of Ahmed's family are crowded round his creation, which has sweet wrappers glittering among the twigs like jewels.

My tree took me and Mark days and days. *It's modern art* he tells me. *It's a sculpture that belongs in a gallery. It's beautiful.* It's just like I knew it would be when I went to Mark's and showed him those two pictures side by side. The golden ratio and the spiral galaxies. The hidden number-letter ciphers. Dots and dashes. My favourite codes.

We have glued together my family. Paintbrushes and glitter tubes and books and Quavers packets and footballs and picture symbols and canvases with Max's drawings of Neil and scribbled paper codes and postcards from Granny M's hometown and pictures of Mum and Dad when they were younger and older stuck to all sides of cardboard boxes that help build the trunk of the tree up and up. We had to build it right here in this hall because there's no way it would fit in our car and it definitely wouldn't fit in Mark's, even with the roof down.

We glued together the objects into spiralling branches and painted them with inky blues and blacks and stuck on pinprick stars made from crisp packets and swirls of universe created from glitter snakes. It's a spiral galaxy of a tree and Mark measured and remeasured and measured again to make sure it matched the measurements of the code to our universe. Our family rippling out and reflecting the whole wide cosmos and the whole wide cosmos reflecting our family.

Mrs Havering let us stay at school extra late yesterday. She was finishing her own tree, hanging a book with the name *Isabel* etched upon the cover in perfect curling script. Next to her name, pinned on the branch of the tree where the cross should be, is a tiny silver heart. I made it for Mrs Havering when I made mine for Mum, and she swept me into her arms in a hug so fierce that it cracked my bones and held me together.

The branches spread out and from them hang all of our stories. Max's has our best photograph stuck on the front, where he has his arms tightly wrapped around my waist and he's not looking at the camera but he's laughing at something that you can't see in the picture. I'm laughing too.

Resting against the trunk of the tree is our family portrait.

I can see Dad and Granny M walking towards me and between them, gripping their hands tightly, is Max. He isn't certain and he is looking out of the sides of his eyes but when he sees me his face splits into a grin and I say out loud

That's my brother.

12 15 22 5

I am eleven and Max is nearly six. I lie
on the floor on my side with Max and
Dad. Between us is his new favourite
spinner which is a Ferris wheel made
from lighting-up sticks that I bought
him from the biggest toy shop in the
world when Granny M and I went
shopping. We spin it together with
our fingers sometimes touching and
catching as the wheel gets faster and
faster and the colours whirl and blur.
The flashes whip past my eyes and I
blink the blotches away but Max keeps
on staring at the wheel. At me. I make a

whooshing noise and Max giggles and our fingers touch again as we whirl the wheel together. Sometimes I touch my nose and Max makes a meep meep noise like I taught him and we all laugh.

Jamie's brother and his dad play PlayStation with Jamie every Sunday night in a death battle competition and they have a league table and everything, but Max and Dad and I lie on the floor and meep and spin spin spin and we walk Neil and we read Max's books and watch films and we get cross and we fall out and then we forget all about it all over again. Dad works

from home for now and I help him sometimes and he's teaching me to write more new codes on my new computer. Max helps to make my robot spin and dance. Dad and I made a game that Max and I can play together and sometimes he wins and sometimes I do. It's not the same as Jamie but it's not that different and it's not anything less at all. We miss Mum but we aren't spinning away and apart into space any more.

Max can be far away in a world all on his own and Max can be right here next to me and Max can be near and far in the same clicked-finger moment. I spin the wheel faster and faster as Max claps his hands and he is here today right now in this moment and I am with him so I can crack his codes and bring him back when he steps into his boat all alone and sails off to the Wild Things. I am his best of all and I am not the Frank who couldn't be brave to Noah and laughed with the boys in the park and I am not poor motherless Frank and I am not part of something falling apart. We are our own spiral galaxy and we are spinning out into the universe and we are made of stardust just like everyone else. The code that holds us together isn't a golden ratio or numbers or taps but it's something bigger and better and harder and more mysterious and beautiful. I reach out through the softly flashing spokes and touch his fingers on purpose this time. Mum was right forever ago when I was five and he was new and nobody knew.

I am Frank and he is Max.

He's my brother.

And it's you, Max, I love.

'It would not be much of a universe if it wasn't home to the people you love'

Stephen Hawking

ACKNOWLEDGEMENTS

Firstly I have to thank my wonderful agent, Catherine Clarke. I was told that she's the best and this is absolutely true. I am so lucky to have you in my corner. I'm also grateful to all of the team at Felicity Bryan Associates and in particular to Jackie Head for scooping me off the submissions pile.

To the absolutely brilliant team at Bloomsbury Children's. Thanks in particular to the best editors in the business, Lucy Mackay-Sim and Rebecca McNally, for taking a tangle of a manuscript and smoothing it into a book, and for being so incredibly kind and sensitive throughout. Sorry about all the WhatsApp pictures of my dog. All writers have a process. To Bea Cross and Jade Westwood for their publicity and marketing wizardry and to Stephanie Amster, Sarah Baldwin, Fliss Stevens, Mary Berry, Anna Swan, Rachael Lucas and Sarah Taylor-Fergusson for their invaluable help.

Thank you to Laura Carlin for her beautiful, sensitive and evocative art throughout the book.

Thanks to kind family – to Helen Cole for looking after the dog even though he's a git, to Toni Boyce for being the best almost-sister, and to Bob Simpson for so much and then an awful lot more. To my friends who variously read my drafts, listened to me whine and offered support, encouragement and the occasional hilarious typo correction: Miranda Prag (my muse), Gaby Aberbach (all those many beautiful days reading children's books!), Theo Whitworth, Clio Seraphim, Cath Newell, Tom Heaton, Sara Halter, Insa Neumann, Laura von Hardenberg, Duncan Willbery and the outrageously kind Claire Wilson. To Leah Carden for the aforementioned typos (though everyone loves a talking dog) and lending her medical expertise, and to Ben Hodgson, who has spent much of his time patiently explaining the golden ratio in the manner a very small child could understand. I think I've nearly got it.

To my 2019 debuts and in particular Savannah Brown, Aisha Bushby, Sam Copeland, Joseph Elliott, Holly Jackson, Sarah Ann Juckes, Struan Murray, Lucy Powrie and Yasmin Rahman.

To all the children, adults and families I have worked with over the years. Frank, Max and their parents may be fictional, but so many strands of them come from you wonderful people and I feel privileged to know you all. For my Mainspringers: I look forward to seeing your work in print and onstage very soon.

To my parents, Malcolm Balen and Karen Meager, for everything. I would be literally and figuratively nothing without you. Thank you thank you thank you. And to my brother, Mischa: I forgive you for selling me my own teddy bear when I was three. You turned out to be a pretty amazing brother. And lawyer.

And finally to Patrick Simpson. I don't think there

can be a kinder, more supportive or more tolerant man in this entire universe of ours. I thank my lucky stars every day.

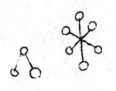

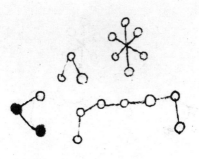

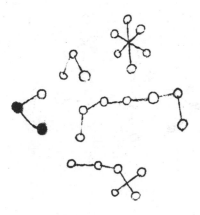

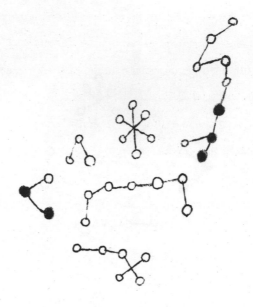